UNCHARTED COUNTRY, UNCERTAIN FUTURE

Sybil Norcroft Book Two

Carl Douglass

Neurosurgeon Turned Author Writes with Gripping Realism

Since
1978

PO Box 221974 Anchorage, Alaska 99522-1974
books@publicationconsultants.com—www.publicationconsultants.com

ISBN 978-1-59433-470-2
eISBN 978-1-59433-471-9
Library of Congress Catalog Card Number: 2014938229

Manufactured in the United States of America.

Dedication

To my family

Disclaimer

The Sybil Series is a work of fiction and should not be construed as representing real persons, places, or events. Some names of real persons and places appear but only for the purpose of creating a setting in the real world or as a mention of historical circumstances. None of the real people or the real places were actually involved in the fictional writing. All of the events described were created from the author's imagination.

Books By Carl Douglass

NONFICTION

Last Phoenix

A Novel of Betrayal and Revenge

All in Jest

Renowned Neurosurgeon in the Fight of Her Life

The Young Coyote

Garven Wilsonhulme's Way to Success—No Quarter Asked
and None Given

Saga of a Neurosurgeon Series, Book One

Anything Goes

Garven Wilsonhulme will do anything and
everything it takes to become a doctor

Saga of a Neurosurgeon Series, Book Two

Heaven and Hell

Garven Wilsonhulme takes on all comers in the jungle of
modern competition

Saga of a Neurosurgeon Series, Book Three

The Long Climb

Young M.D., Garven Wilsonhulme, engaged
in a social poker game of winner takes all

Saga of a Neurosurgeon Series, Book Four

ACADEMIA: The Law of the Jungle

Surgeon in training, Garven Wilsonhulme, fang-and-claw competition for glory

Saga of a Neurosurgeon Series, Book Five

The Vulture and the Phoenix

Neurosurgeon, Garven Wilsonhulme, the final great fight

Saga of a Neurosurgeon Series, Book Six

Finders Keepers, Losers Weep

A Novel of Innocence Betrayed and the Search for Restitution

Gog and Magog

Yawm al-Qiyamah, Yawm al-Din The Day of Judgment
Sheep Dog and the Wolf
A Story of Terrorism and Response, and the Sheep
Dogs Who Protect
Though They Come from the Ends of the Earth
A Novel of the Iran Nuclear Weapons Interdiction Project
Book One of the Trojan Horse in the Belly of the Beast Trilogy
Dancing with the Devil
A Novel of the Iran Nuclear Weapons Interdiction Project
Book Two of the Trojan Horse in the Belly of the Beast Trilogy
The Trojan Horse in the Belly of the Beast
A Novel of the Iran Nuclear Weapons Interdiction Project
Book Three of the Trojan Horse in the Belly of
the Beast Trilogy
The End of the Beginning
Sybil Norcroft Book One
Uncharted Country, Uncertain Future
Sybil Norcroft Book Two
Secrets
Sybil Norcroft Book Three
Secrets and Scandals
Sybil Norcroft Book Four
Decisions
Sybil Norcroft Book Five
Running with the Big Dogs
Sybil Norcroft Book Six
NONFICTION
On Evolution
The Origin of Selection, Order, Progression, and Diversity
Out osf print
Something About Religion
Out osf print

Chapter One

The Wolf News main studio was in a state of controlled pandemonium—not the usual beehive of activity at the change of shifts, but an all-out effort to capitalize on breaking news that would give them some one-upmanship over the arch-rival WWN. The latest war in the DRC [Democratic Republic of the Congo] had taken a particularly ugly turn in the form of a medical and humanitarian disaster somewhat similar to that of the Rwanda genocide of two decades previously. WWN had the upper-hand among news crews in the western provinces of the DRC where large-scale battles were raging and upon which the world's attention was focused. Wolf News was relegated to playing second-fiddle and had to get most of its news footage from friendly—but expensive—Reuters News Service teams.

Wolf got wind of another compelling story—one occurring far away from the main western offensives—which was taking place in the eastern Congolese province of North-Kivu. The information came from a disgruntled former WWN reporter, Jules Renier, who was witness to unspeakable atrocities being perpetrated by the Mayi-Mavi Cheka and M23 [March 23 Movement] rebels in the jungle border country area of the DRC, Uganda, Burundi, and Rwanda. Because of the wars, atrocities, and neglect by the country's government, the unfortunate civilians of the region were experiencing an unprecedented scourge of combined and serial epidemics of sleeping sickness, yaws, malaria, and cholera which compounded the already second highest infant mortality rate in the world. The most compelling aspect of Renier's report was that pygmy people of the area were being subjected to medical experimentations using highly infectious disease agents. Renier was adamant about secrecy. He did not want to see Raja Patel and the WWN news hordes descending into his village and taking all of the credit.

The executives were caught up in a frenzied effort to get there first and with the most. Into this maelstrom stepped the newest Wolf reporter, a woman hired to counter the engaging and hugely successful WWN medical reportage featuring their star, Raja Patel, M.D., part-time neurosurgeon and researcher at Cornell University and media darling. The new "reporter"—more accurately, medical consultant—was Sybil Norcroft, M.D., Ph.D., F.A.C.S., associate professor of neurosurgery at Georgetown University School of Medicine and former highly prominent neurosurgeon in California. Much of her notoriety stemmed from her highly touted and well-publicized work with LGBT groups, Latino organizations, the National Women-in-Medicine Organization, American College of Surgeons, the American Association of Neurological Surgeons, and the Congress of Neurosurgeons. If the truth were fully known, her stardom really stemmed from a recent case in which she had been tried and dramatically acquitted for the murder of a malpractice attorney who had tormented her for years. The impression all over the United States was that she had been the victim of sexism, and she had become the face of the ongoing fight against gender bias. It did not hurt that she was a photogenic, beautiful, statuesque, blond, genius with remarkable stage presence.

David Kilcannon, vice-president of Wolf News production for the channel, met Sybil as she walked into the lobby of Wolf News headquarters on the Avenue of the Americas in New York. He was a little breathless from the hectic start of his day. Sybil—on the other hand—was the very picture of poise and calm. She was dressed in a beautiful pearl-grey Italian Valentino pantsuit, Gucci high heels, and was carrying a Fendi handbag from Paris. She was perfectly coiffed; and— all-in-all—was the picture of cool worldly haute couture.

David rushed up to Sybil and extended his hand.

"I'm David Kilcannon, vice-president of news coverage here, Sybil. Okay if I call you Sybil?"

"Certainly," the vision in grey replied and favored him with a fulsome smile.

"Sorry, Sybil, but we don't have any time for formalities and certainly not for niceties. I know you came to prepare our introductory interview with Barbara Welhelme for welcome to Wolf, but something has come up that trumps that. We need you to go to work today. In the Congo…"

"Are you serious!?" she asked. "I don't think I came dressed for the Congo."

"Indeed you're not. We'll get you over to the REI and outfitted. It is a jungle there—no joke intended—and you need the right stuff. I want to send you and a photographer and two staffers to the Democratic Republic of the Congo to do an exclusive story. You won't have a script or make-up people. You have a great reputation for thinking on your feet, and this will be your baptism by fire in that regard. You up to a new life of adventure?"

Without the slightest hesitation, Sybil answered, "I am. Let's get started."

David grinned partly in satisfaction and partly in relief.

"Okay, I'll go with you and fill you in on the details as we go."

He was altogether true to his word, continuing his patter as the elegant and sophisticated beauty shed her haute couture for tough camouflage BDUs, jungle boots, and an assortment of sunscreens and bug repellents. She bought ballistic nylon duffle bags and a large carry-on messenger bag. She made even that combat attire look fetching. She laughed at herself in the mirror. She called her husband, Charles Daniels, in his Georgetown satellite office of his international agri-business of which he was the CEO and filled him in. He sighed and wished her fair winds and a following sea and demanded that she come back to him in one piece.

The last preparation of the morning was to get her a Glock .30 handgun and ammunition, SWAT team quality pepper spray, and a combat knife—all of which were ensconced in her check-in luggage. The Wolf team had thought of just about everything. Sybil had a suite of rooms in the Marriott Marque; and, with her full consent, they fetched her passport and other necessaries that she kept in the hotel room's safe. David gave her $100,000 in small denomination bills, a black credit card with no limit, and the latest, greatest in satellite phones. He and several assistants put her and her team on a first-class flight to Kinshaha—with stops in London and Pretoria—at two o'clock New York time. She had reading material to bring her fully up to speed on the developing situation in the eastern DRC. Aside from being on her way to what she could only regard as uncharted country and an uncertain future, Sybil Norcroft could hardly contain her excitement at the once-in-a-lifetime opportunity that had just fallen into her lap.

She and her team landed at N'Djili and Kinshasa International Airport for their last layover and then flew in a Hewa Bora Airways DC-9 puddle-jumper to Goma, the capital of North Kivu province—a city with a million inhabitants plunked squarely in the heart of the rain forest. They were numb with exhaustion and had to sleep for 18 hours in their Ihusi Hotel suite to recuperate enough to function. While sitting down for breakfast—their first real meal in 56 hours—they met Jules Renier. He ate with them and studiously avoided talking news business until they could find an empty conference room where he brought them up-to-date as of the present hour.

"Glad you're here and that you're young and healthy, unlike me. I am not up to this whole thing. Good you're a doctor, Sybil, the uninitiated would not be able to handle what you're going to see."

Sybil and her team listened raptly and worked to hide their reactions to Renier's shocking revelations.

"To say that there are unimaginable atrocities going on by the rebels is the mastery of understatement," he said. "I'm going to take you to a little town in North-Kivu called Rutshuru located between Lakes Edward and Kivu. It is deep in the jungle only a few miles either way from Uganda and Rwanda and was the scene of horrors during the Rwandan massacres of the nineties. There is all of that again, but that is only part of the story. The main thing—and I don't think any western news agency knows about—is what has been happening to the pygmies."

He showed them photographs he had taken that would have turned the stomachs of less experienced viewers. The clincher—and one which he was not certain of the cause—was of bloated corpses of tiny pygmies—men, women, and children—covered with bleeding sores and obviously grossly enlarged lymph nodes.

"It's anybody's guess what this is, but I am almost certain that the Fabrique Pharmaceutique DRC is responsible."

Sybil said quietly, "I think I know what it is. Ebola."

Renier and the Wolf team all cringed at the word.

After a moment's pause to contemplate what they were being told, the Wolf News crew heard Renier out for the rest of his description.

He concluded by telling them, "I have three Range Rovers and a good map for you. My guys have packed some grenades, two LAWs rocket launchers, two hazmat suits for each team member, several large trunks full of medical supplies, and MRE field rations for food in the vehicles. This is tiger country, my friends; you will likely need most of this stuff. The tigers are M23 and the Mayi-Mavi Cheka. You be very, very careful. I am too old for this sort of thing anymore, and I will stay back here in Goma to relay messages and to get any supplies you might need to you. Good luck. You'll need it."

The dirt roads were slick with mud in spots, but the sturdy vehicles carried Sybil's crew to Rutshuru safely. They did not encounter any rebel bands, a fact that lifted their spirits considerably. Any good feelings they had evaporated when they drove into the nearly deserted village.

Chapter Two

A mile past the pharmaceutical company's factory build-ings, they saw a few dazed people milling about an open building. There was no mistaking what the people were looking at. The stench of death coming from the building was all the evidence they needed to assure them that they were in the right place. Evan Crutchfield and Doug Mason, the photographers, jumped out of the Range Rovers and began to take movies and digital stills of the most horrifying scene Sybil had ever seen. She had once thought that her experience in training of dealing with murder victims had been the refiners' fire for her, but this transcended anything she could have imagined. The open-air building held row upon row of neatly laid out bodies of diminutive people, the majority of which were tiny children. She counted nearly 150 of them. The bodies had not been mutilated by any kind of war atrocities. They were covered with large bloody sores and copious evidence of hemorrhagic vomiting and diarrhea. They all had a raised violaceous rash, obvious severe weight loss, and the remnants of bleeding from their noses, mouths, rectums, eyes, and ears.

Sybil collected herself, put a large swath of mentholatum under her nose, and then directed the photographers to film her against the backdrop of macabre horror. She introduced herself and told the unseen audience—which would soon see for themselves the dreadful scene—that this was her first day as a Wolf News medical correspondent, and that this was the worst example of man's inhumanity to man she had ever seen. She quoted the on-lookers—who were similarly afflicted by what had destroyed the lives of the poor victims lying in the building—who told her in French that the hazmat suited people from the Fabrique Pharmaceutique DRC had rounded them up and injected something into their veins. Within a week, they all started to have fever, excruciating headaches, joint and muscle aches, chills, horribly sore throats, and severe progressive weakness. Pointing at the shed, they wept and said that they were the walking dead, just like their friends and family who were finally out of their misery.

"Our investigation is just beginning, but every evidence points to Fabrique Pharmaceutique DRC and its CEO, Damien de Gaulle. We will make every effort to track this man down and to assist the PNC [Congolese National Police] government security forces to bring him and every other person involved to justice," Sybil said and finished her first report for national television.

The footage was e-mailed back to New York for release on prime time that evening.

The few remaining pygmy people left in the village were now sitting listlessly on the ground. Sybil asked if there were any survivors and learned that most of the people had fled into the jungles on the Nyamuragira and Mavi Ya Moto volcanoes. Did they know where the factory people were? Most of them just shrugged, but one older man—a four-foot-tall, almost naked community elder—told her about a village called Sanchia located 15 km to the west in Rwanda where he thought they had gone. When the factory people left Rutshuru, they had taken boxes of medicine which he thought might be the infective agent and some intravenous antibiotics the factory had been making.

"Let's go see if we can locate the pygmies and try and help them first, then we should concentrate on the factory people who pose a huge potential threat to the world," Sybil said.

She was by then accepted as the undisputed leader of the crew, and they were all glad to have a firm hand guiding them. They drove to the point that the roads became tracks—barely passable—and finally to where there were nothing but foot or mule trails. They found a guide and hiked the last several miles through the steaming jungle to a pitiful encampment of what appeared to be nearly starving pygmies. The guide served to introduce them as friends, and the extremely wary pygmies were willing to accept them.

The Wolf crew gathered as much information and photographic evidence as they could, and filmed the second in their series of reports for the channel. The humble pygmy victims gathered around the reporters in curiosity, having never seen anything remotely like the technology the strangers brought in.

Sybil made a heartfelt request of the world outside the rainforest where she was standing, "Please send emergency help of every kind to these hapless little people. They have been abused for centuries starting with the Belgians. During the first two, and now this, the third, Congo Civil War, they have been subject to mass rape and other sexual violence, torture, enslavement, and murder. This unfortunate country has seen nearly six million of its people die during the conflicts. They need help, and they need it now."

With that, she closed the segment, and the team headed back down the mountain. They camped sleeping on the hard ground and got up during the pre-dawn darkness of the next morning and following their map by flashlight, made their way towards the village of Sanchia. Sybil contacted Jules Renier in Goma and asked him to get the PNC up there to try and capture the pharmaceutical company's executives and to round up as many of their murderous coconspirators as possible.

"Look here, Sybil," Jules said. "You are not the army. Even they can't do what you asked. If you go up there, you won't accomplish a thing except to get killed. Plant yourself right where you are. Pitch a tent; read a book; play pinochle or whatever. I'll get you some help, but not quite the invasion of Normandy you seem to be envisioning."

Sybil realized that she was being overzealous and was probably endangering her crew; so, she agreed to wait.

"Not too long," she said.

Twelve hours later, a battered old Range Rover pulling a small trailer drove up to where they were camped. It was still light; and, as they had done all day, the Wolf crew had posted two sentries serving to communicate with the rest of the people in the small encampment and as front-line defense. The vehicle disgorged its lone occupant who walked into the camp apparently unarmed as if he belonged there.

Sybil greeted the tall, wiry newcomer calmly. He was dressed in old khaki shorts and a tattered but fairly clean military brownish tee shirt and hiking boots. He wore aviator sunglasses and cut a dashing figure out there in the bush that was almost laughable. Doug and Evan started to take his photograph, but he moved with surprising alacrity to stop them.

"No pics, please," he said, "I am a secret agent and would have to shoot you."

He smiled with his lips, but not with his eyes; and it was not so clear that he was joking.

"I'm John Smith, CIA," he said.

Everybody laughed, including him. The CIA undoubtedly paid for the services of several thousand John Smiths. He flashed a cred pack quickly enough that no one could see his real identity, but the credentials looked genuine enough otherwise.

"So, you're from the government, and you've come to help," Sybil quipped.

"In a manner of speaking. I am on your side, and I have a certain skill set and some resources that might be of benefit in your current undertaking. Let's talk."

The crew told John everything they knew and asked for his help for when they got to Sanchia.

He said, "I saw the massacre back there in Rutshuru. Looks like mass torture, but not the regular kind. The Firm would love to bring this guy in. We have a pretty good working relationship with the PNC, but they are largely engaged elsewhere for the moment. It will be up to us to find this monster, de Gaulle, and persuade him to come out with us. I'm afraid we won't be able to bring all of them in. I saw your piece from yesterday in the village which indicated that you think that they have an intentionally inflicted massacre by Ebola and that the perpetrators have a supply that they intend to use someplace else. That has to be our priority. Arrests, courts, justice, and payback will just have to wait their turn, okay?"

The Wolf crew nodded their understanding and agreement in unison.

During the dim light of that day's gloaming, they drove to within a kilometer of Sanchia village and parked off in the trees. John, Sybil, and the crew armed themselves with military materiel and camera supplies and trudged to the margins of the village and the jungle on foot. Sybil was excited, more excited than she could ever remember being.

John was now the nominal head of the small group. He had obvious military or CIA paramilitary experience, and no one—including Sybil—felt it necessary to challenge his implicit authority. He put up his hand to get the crew to stay in the safety of the tall rainforest trees, then he slid into the village under cover of the gathering darkness. He was gone for a nervous thirty minutes before he appeared out of nowhere behind them. Sybil thought her heart would leap out of her chest.

He pulled her close to him and whispered very quietly, "I think he's here. We'll have to wait until they get altogether drunk and pass out before we go after him or else none of us will get out of this little jungle hell-hole alive. Take it easy. We'll go in about two in the morning."

They got some sleep until the CIA agent roused them. They all—including Sybil—put on a belt with a handgun and a crisscross set of bandoliers—one for grenades and the other for ammunition for the AR-15s each of them hefted, and military grade night vision goggles. The darkness enveloped them; but the luminescent green view through the goggles made the going easy.

John was in front. He suddenly stopped and held up his right hand. Everyone else froze.

Without saying a word, John took five steps forward and through his arm around the neck of the first sentry they encountered. The sentry was one of the factory workers who certainly could have intimidated and abused the little pygmy people, but he was no match for John. The agent broke the sentry's neck as easily as if he were dispatching a chicken. He signaled for them to move forward again.

In front of them was a row of six thatch-roofed huts which were fairly sturdily constructed. There were no more guards that anyone could see at the moment; so, they followed John to the third hut in the row and paused at the door and under the frameless windows. They listened intently but only the sound of some soft snoring and a few turnings in bed—apparently on straw-tic mattresses—emanated from the one room cabin. John pulled Sybil, Evan, and Doug close to him and whispered as softly as possible but enough; so, they could each hear.

"Third bed from our left. He has a big belly. The rest are pretty small, and one of them is a girl—probably a pygmy or a bantu child forced to service the men. This has to be silent, or we are going to be in the fight of our lives. I'll take de Gaulle. Sybil, you take the girl because she could make a high-pitched scream. Evan and Doug, take the other two."

"Define 'take'," Sybil asked.

"Have your knife out, but put a hand over your target's mouth and tell them to keep quiet or die. If they struggle or try to sound an alarm, do what you have to do."

Sybil thought to herself, "*Two days ago, I was a high fashion about-to-be-media star, never did a violent thing in my whole life, and now I may have to kill a person, even a poor girl. What on earth have I gotten myself into?*" Then she thought back to the rows of little pygmy corpses and steeled her nerves, "*little brothers and sisters, this is for you.*"

"At my count down from three," John said.

The agent and the Wolf crew were standing over their targets who were still sound asleep with heavy vapors of alcohol on their breaths.

John whispered, "Three, two, one…" and in what seemed like a well-choreographed set of movements, every target had a strong hand on his or her mouth, a knife point digging into his or her neck, and was intimidated into a terrified silence.

The little girl let out a moan of muffled terror.

"Shh, little one," Sybil whispered soothingly to her. "You are safe. Keep quiet. I won't hurt you."

She said it in French presuming that it was the lingua franca between them.

John whispered to Sybil, "Bring the girl to me and get the duct tape out of my rook sack. We'll secure the men and take the girl with us. She's been through enough.

Sybil told her what was going to happen and to stay quiet, and she would be all right. They quickly put duct tape strips on the mouths and eyes of the targets and bound their wrists. John left first with the girl, then the others followed into the blackness. The girl had calmed down—hoping against hope—that this was not to be just another night of horror. Doug and Evan picked up two large cardboard boxes full of medicine vials and carried them under their arms.

At first Damien de Gaulle tried to struggle and to impede progress, but a few well-aimed kicks and punches convinced him that further efforts would be futile, and maybe fatal. He was attached to John's waist by a nylon rope and grimly trotted along behind him with his hands in front of his face to protect against branches. He stumbled and staggered since he did not have the benefit of night vision goggles like his captors, but he kept up fairly well.

They loaded themselves and their captive back into the Range Rovers and drove back down the mountain track without turning on their headlights. It was slow going, almost as much by feel as by sight. At the outskirts of Rutshuru village the first hints of daylight began to appear. John had them halt.

"If the villagers see that we have de Gaulle with us, they are likely to mob us and tear him limb from limb and probably us as well."

He turned to the girl, and, speaking in fluent French asked her if she wanted to be let off in the village or to go with the rescue team.

"To Paris?" she asked.

Sybil said, "No, sweetheart, to America."

America was a dream more than a real place to the plucky child, but she replied, "with you" without hesitation. It seemed to Sybil that she had just adopted an exotic child. The more she thought about it, the more she liked the idea.

They crept through the town and saw no one. By the time it was light, they pulled over to stop and take a drink and have some beef jerky. The girl ate her share with gusto and grinned her pleasure. Damien de Gaulle nibbled cautiously, sure that he was being poisoned. Doug and Evan took pictures of themselves, Sybil, the girl—who by now they had learned was named Cerisse Monet—and the frowning captive, who kept trying to hide his face from the cameras. Neither photographer made any attempt to get a picture of the CIA agent.

They rumbled and bumped over the poor substitute for a road back towards Goma. Two miles out, they encountered a road block. John wheeled his Range Rover around in an expert bootlegger's turn and led the three vehicle convoy back the way they came. They were too late. The Sanchia villagers had awakened and radioed ahead. Their confederates in Goma had reacted with speed and good planning. Two more vehicles pulled across the road behind John and Sybil's convoy. John stopped.

"Stay inside," he said. "The trucks are mostly bullet proof. Keep your heads down and your guns up. This is going to get ugly."

Sybil—the new mom—pushed her frightened little charge down onto the floor between the seats. Her adrenaline was pumping so hard, that she had no thought about the danger, but focused only on the enemy, her gun, and the critical little girl she had chosen to adopt. She was also grimly determined to protect the crucial evidence contained in the cardboard boxes.

AK-47 rounds began to kick up dust plumes all around the Range Rovers. The shooting was meant to intimidate them but not to take a risk on killing their boss as collateral damage. John watched carefully as two heads popped up from behind the open doors of the old Toyota trucks—the favorite vehicles of terrorists all over the world. He set his AR-15 to a fire a short burst of three rounds every time he squeezed the trigger and fired in a small sweeping motion. Two voices cried out in French and then became silent. John whirled about and squeezed his trigger three times in rapid succession with his bullets punching holes through the windows of the two trucks blocking their escape to the rear. The stand-off became quiet.

"Give us de Gaulle and the medicine boxes, and you get to leave alive. You know you can't outwait us. We have all year," a hoarse French voice called to them.

"Nuts!" John yelled. He turned to Sybil and said, "I been waiting forever to say that—remember General Anthony McAuliffe's reply to the Nazi's demand that he surrender when he was hopelessly out numbered during a WW II battle?" he asked Sybil.

Sybil rolled her eyes, "I do, the Battle of Bulge," she said and smiled at the flamboyant CIA agent.

"What means, 'nuts'?" the Frenchman yelled, obviously confused.

"No head for history," John said to Sybil.

She laughed.

"I have a plan," John said.

"That's reassuring…I think," Sybil said. "Let's hear it."

Chapter Three

They whispered. He called the men in the other two Range Rovers, and they agreed. On John's count of three, all of the men and Sybil began firing in what the military call a "mad minute." While the firing continued, John rolled out of the vehicle and ran as fast as his legs would carry him in the direction of the vehicles blocking the road leading towards Goma. He zigzagged in a wide serpentine series of arcs until he was almost to the vehicles. A head popped up, and John shot a hole in its forehead. Two others popped up and fired wildly with their AK-47s in the general direction of where they had last heard John's shooting. He was not there, and they died for their mistake.

He ran alongside one of the Toyotas and dropped a grenade through the open window. He was behind the second truck before it went off. Four men clambered out of that truck and aimed at John. Sybil, Doug, and Evan opened fire on them, and they went down. John lobbed another grenade into the truck and began zigzagging his way back towards his own truck.

Sybil drove towards the remaining two Toyotas and the second Range Rover drove alongside of her. They were traveling forty-miles-per-hour when they hit the two parked trucks. Fabrique Pharmaceutique DRC men scrambled out of the wreckage and tried to shoot, but they were too shaken to be dangerous. Sybil shot two of them; and Doug got another; but the fourth came running in a maniacal dash towards Sybil's vehicle door.

She was out of ammunition, and neither Doug nor Evan could get of a shot without hitting Sybil. She threw caution out the door with her and parried the advancing killer's knife arm off to his left. She made a well-practiced Brazilian Jiu Jitsu move which caught the surprised assassin's arm with a twist that put Sybil's arm around his in a hold that bent him over and snapped his arm into an unnatural angle at the elbow. He went down with a scream of pain, and Sybil kicked him square in the face with the side of her jungle boot, and he fell in a silent heap on the ground.

John, Doug, and Evan looked at her in consternation, astonishment, and then admiration.

"That was a real hotchaa move, young lady. I take it that was not a fluke."

"No, it was thanks to ten years of training from Pedro Sauer. It seems to have paid off."

Cerisse ran to Sybil and hugged her leg with a ferocious clasp. Sybil returned the gesture, and they held each other for almost a minute.

"Oh," Cerisse said, "I forgot in the excitement. The bad man—de Gaulle—he ran away. He took the boxes with him."

Sybil and the men groaned. As they did, they saw a fifth Toyota truck churning up dust on its way into Goma.

"He can't get away," Sybil screamed and raced for one of the Range Rovers.

Cerisse and Doug went with her, and John and Evan got into one of the other Range Rovers. They dodged around the two destroyed Toyota trucks and drove as fast as possible into Goma, but de Gaulle's truck and his biological weapons of mass destruction were gone from sight.

Sybil called Jules, and John called his CIA counterparts in Goma, and soon there was a dragnet out for the CEO. As soon as they thought about it and began to race towards one of the city's small plane airports, they saw a piper cub take off towards the southwest.

"Too late," Sybil moaned in defeat.

"Maybe not. Fabrique Pharmaceutique DRC has its headquarters in Goma, and de Gaulle has a house and a wife here. I know where both of them are," Jules said; and another race was on.

There was nothing at the office to help them; so, everyone piled back into the now many vehicles and raced to de Gaulle's home. Two CIA agents crashed in the door, and the small army entered guns drawn. There was no sign of de Gaulle, but his terrified wife—when threatened with a long incognito stay in one of Goma's infamous jails—coughed up the information that her husband was on his way to Washington D. C. His American Airlines flight was to go via London and Frankfurt and then on to IAD [Washington-Dulles International Airport]. So far as she knew, the passengers would not be able to get off the plane during the stops.

Back in their Range Rovers, John called Langley to get a private company jet from Kinshasa to Paris and then on to Washington.

"Central Intelligence Agency of the United States, how may I direct your call?"

He entered his ID number followed by his password and security clearance identifier.

"Office of the Assistant Director. How may I help you, agent?"

"I have an urgent emergency that threatens the national security. I need to have the DDCIA okay a private Company plane from Paris to D.C. I must make the flight no later than three hours from now."

"I will see if he is available. Please stay on the line."

Three minutes elapsed.

"I am sorry, sir. The assistant director is in a national security council and cannot be disturbed. Please leave a number where you can be reached."

"This is a national security issue of the first order. Please get the man on the phone or get me the director himself."

The line clicked dead.

"He wouldn't talk to me, and his secretary hung up on me!" John said, fuming.

"Let me make a try," Sybil said.

She dialed in the required numbers.

"Hello, do you realize that this a private secure line?" Charles Daniels's familiar voice came through.

"I do, my love. I am in trouble, and I need your help."

"Sybil! Where are you? I have been worried sick."

"I'm in the Congo. I have lots of news but no time. I need for you to authorize a private company plane to take me and two other people from Paris to Washington D.C. I have to leave Paris three hours from now. Okay? By the way, I have just scored the scoop of all time. Turn on Wolf News, and you can follow my progress. And, also by the way, I adopted a little girl."

"And I take that you don't have time to tell me all about all of that?"

"Nope. Some of it is a national security secret, and the other will take a while to tell. Please, Charles."

"Consider it done. Why don't you get a flight with Wolf News credit card?"

"Too slow. Thanks, love. See you later."

And she hung up.

Next she called David Kilcannon.

"Hi, David, it's Sybil."

"You're sending us great stuff, keep it coming."

"I have more. I am in hot pursuit of the CEO of Fabrique Pharmaceutique DRC. He has a box of vials of what I am pretty sure is either Ebola or Marburg or both. I am not certain what he intends to do with it, but I am fairly sure he intends to do it in Washington. I need you to have a fast limo at the arrival area. My pilot will keep you posted about our arrival time."

"I'll take care of it. Keep the good stuff rolling. Hey, you didn't mention your team. Are they with you?"

"Nope, I had to leave them in Kinshasa. They will make their way back to the states. Don't expect them for a couple of days. Doug and Evan have some great footage for you to go over. I hope to get more stuff in the next 24 hours. I'll keep you posted."

"What about your big introductory interview? Any idea when you will be available?"

"By the end of the week. Let all of this settle down and for the stories to gel first. See you in the Big Apple in a day or two. Thanks for the help."

The Argos Daniels Mitzuki Global Company jet was waiting for the Wolf News consultant, her new daughter, and the CIA agent at the Charles de Gaulle International Airport. Certain adjustments had been made to accommodate the powerful American and Japanese global food-processing and commodities-trading corporation. The formalities of customs and passport checks were bypassed, and their luggage was in the cargo bay of the Gulfstream V jet before the passengers could fasten their seat belts. Charles and his company bought the luxurious plane because of its ultra-long-range capability.

"Having fun, Cerisse?" Sybil asked the adoring little girl with eyes as wide as saucers.

"It is most lovely," the excited child said, hardly able to keep her seat due to all of the sensory input.

Cerisse had never seen a passenger plane up close or been inside one, let alone be a passenger. She thought that this must be how you get to heaven.

They touched down at Dulles three and a half hours later and were whisked away in the Wolf News limo.

"We need to get to the FBI building as fast as you can get us there," Sybil said to the driver.

"You got it, Dr. Norcroft. Mr. Kilcannon said I should take you wherever you want and wait as long as you want."

"That's nice of him and you. I forgot to ask, what is your name?"

No one had ever asked his name before.

"Dave. Dave Fulbright, Ma'am."

"If you don't mind, I would rather you didn't call me 'Ma'am'. It kind of chafes me. Call me Dr. Norcroft or Sybil if you prefer."

"Thanks. That's nice."

Sybil noticed that the limo speeded up a bit after the conversation.

When they stopped by the J. Edgar Hoover FBI Building, Cerisse was dumbfounded. It was the largest building she had ever seen.

"Cerisse, honey, would you please go with this nice man. He is going to take you to my office, and a nice lady and her husband will take you home until I can get my business done. Okay?"

Cerisse looked stricken as if she had just suffered another of the legions of betrayals and abuses which characterized her short 14 years of life. She started to sob.

"I thought you loved me. Now you're going to sell me?" she blurted out, devastated.

"Oh, baby, no, no, no. I love you. You will always be my daughter. I am sorry that you could even think such a thing. You don't have to go. Stay with me and be my partner. You are safe. I will protect you as long as I live."

Cerisse still looked unsure and insecure, but she trotted along beside Sybil almost touching her all the way. John Smith—real name Edgar Simonsen—thought he might cry as he watched the distress suffered by the terribly mistreated girl and the salvation that Sybil represented. He vowed to remember the remarkable woman. She was going to be important in this city one day.

They were directed to the office of national security investigations where they met with the director of the section. Simonsen and Norcroft tag-teamed smoothly to tell the story and what they were doing.

"This is Cerisse, who was a slave of de Gaulle's in every way you can imagine," Sybil told him. "She can identify him better than anyone else alive. We are taking her with us."

"Could get dicey for a little girl," Director Holdaway said.

"You can't even imagine what this child has seen and experienced. There can't be anything on the horizon more 'dicey' than she has already experienced. She is smart, brave, and tough. I will take care of her."

Holdaway shrugged.

In half an hour, a joint force of CIA, FBI, and CDC [Center for Disease Control] Special Pathogens and Bacteria Branch agents was assembled to begin the manhunt. They brought in infectious disease and chemical weapons experts and made ready the appropriate hazmat vehicles, labs, and equipment. A federal BOLO went out to every law enforcement office, post office, and public service building in the nation. The assistant director called his counterpart in France for help in Europe and in the DRC, which is the most officially francophone country in the world outside of France. They all agreed that the most difficult element in their manhunt was trying to guess what the terrorists' target was and when the attack might take place.

There was nothing more to do; so, Simonsen and Norcroft parted ways agreeing to meet at her office at the Wolf News building the next morning. They had stopped playing the charade of him being "John Smith" on the flight to Washington.

Chapter Four

Sybil presented Cerisse to Charles. Charles stepped toward the timid little girl to give her a hug, but she recoiled and backed away to where she could feel Sybil's body next to hers. Charles knelt down and quietly—speaking French in dulcet tones—coaxed her to come to him. He gently touched her shoulders. She came a bit closer. He put his arms very lightly around her thin thorax and kissed her forehead.

"*Bienvenue*! [Welcome]," he said.

She looked at the big white man with her doe eyes, and began to cry. The floodgates of a lifetime emptied her reservoir. Charles held her close to him and let her cry it all out. She could not have been four feet tall or weighed more than seventy pounds. He was six foot four and weighed a muscular 280 pounds. Now, instead of being afraid, Cerisse melted into the safety and comfort of the giant man, the first one who had ever treated her with kindness without next forcing her to have sex with him.

Sybil was exhausted, and she allowed her pent-up emotions to overflow as well. The three of them became a bonded family during that meeting.

Sybil called David Kilcannon then Edgar Simonsen who brought her up to date. Simonsen told her that they had found the dead body of Damien de Gaulle in an apartment in Tysons Corners early that morning. He had the early signs of Ebola/Marburg disease, and apparently had a heart attack. The virulent bacteria and their antidote were missing.

"Where does that leave us?" Sybil as the CIA operative.

"Close to being back to square one. We need to regroup and make some decisions. You know I can't have any visible involvement on American soil; so, I guess you will mostly have to work with Special Agent Zacharia Nichols who has been running point. He's easy to work with unlike most fibbies and is willing to include you in the decision making group to a certain point. He even said he was willing to share the spotlight if you cooperate; but if you make unapproved TV statements, he will cut you off from any involvement in a second."

"Sounds fair. What's next?"

A meeting at noon in the Hoover building. Nichols's office is on the fifth floor—542. Just check in at the reception desk. They will be expecting you."

Sybil got Cerisse off to a test run at the very exclusive and expensive Georgetown Visitation Preparatory School. The headmistress, Dr. Stephanie Bradshaw, agreed to take the pygmy girl in for at least a day or two to get some idea of how she could be educated given the deprivation she had experienced thus far in her life. Cerisse was thrilled to be around so many bright, happy, and friendly girls—black, white, brown, and yellow girls, it made no difference. She understood that Sybil would be back to get her at the end of the school day, and that she was safe within the confines of the school buildings and the grounds. It helped that she spoke fluent French, and that she was intelligent. Sybil felt hopeful as she raced in her BMW from Georgetown to the District to the FBI building.

Agent Simonsen met her at the door to room 542 and introduced her to Special Agent Nichols. In a few minutes of conversation they became Ed, Zach, and Sybil. A younger female agent gave a brief and to-the-point presentation of the status of the investigation and pursuit from its inception in the Congo until the death scene in Tysons Corner the previous night.

Zach asked, "Anything on the boxes de Gaulle was carrying?"

"Nothing specific on them, but a quick lab check by CDC established that we are dealing with MHF [Marburg hemorrhagic fever]. As infectious diseases go, this is about the worst there is—deadly, highly infections—case fatality rate approaching 90%—and not altogether obvious in a modestly clothed individual until late in the disease. Both Marburg and Ebola are rare, and both have a ready capacity to cause dramatic outbreaks with high fatality rates. The CDC has had experience in Africa and Europe with monkey-to-human and human-to-human spread. So far as we know, there is no specific antiviral treatment or vaccine available as of this date.

The CDC has projection studies that indicate that Marburg or its first cousin, Ebola, can spread at the rate of dozens from one infected person growing into thousands, and maybe hundreds of thousands or even millions within a month or so and would probably be even worse if a weaponized virus were used. The USSR had three plants that are known to have produced weaponized virus; and, for all we know, the plants are still producing such viruses; but the Russians insist they are only for defensive purposes. Take that any way you want."

Special Agent Nichols said, "Let's hear from the CDC first, then I'd like to hear from Dr. Norcroft, a clinician who seems to be eminently capable of thinking on the run. And—bear in mind—with the potential super epidemic we could be facing, we are on the run. Dr. Thomas."

Cecil Thomas, Ph.D., head of the slow virus lab at the CDC, stood up and started his laptop PowerPoint program on MHF. He talked rapidly as he went.

"Here are some key bits of information about this dangerous pathogen:

"It is a genetically unique RNA filovirus classified by WHO [the World Health Organization] as a risk group four pathogen requiring intensive biosafety containment. It is dependent on an animal host to continue its existence. There is ample evidence in bats, monkeys, pigs, and humans that infection and reinfection cycles amplify the potency and infectivity of the virus.

"It is mainly transmitted human-to-human. The transmission includes needle sticks, semen—so it can be considered an STD—and even close contact with bodily secretions or infected organs. Health-care workers are at significant risk. In fact, needle stick transmission is extremely effective and produces more virulent disease than other sources.

"The virus can persist for upwards of seven weeks in infected people who do not succumb to the disease; so, semen becomes a reservoir for perpetuation of an epidemic.

"Direct contact with the bodies of persons who die from the infection, such as in burial ceremonies or expressions of grief in which mourners touch exposed skin have been significant in the spread. Health-care workers who do not use protection are well-known to assist spread.

"Signs and symptoms: The incubation period varies from 2 to 21 days, and is quicker in weaponized virus transmissions. The disease presents itself abruptly and without prodrome. There is usually high fever, severe headache, malaise—enervating flu-like symptoms—muscle aches, severe watery diarrhea—which the Chinese call 'rice-water diarrhea—violent abdominal pain and cramping, nausea and vomiting, and a very prominent but non-itchy rash. The appearance of patients at this phase is characteristic and frightening for the uninitiated and superstitious—"ghost-like" drawn features, deep-set eyes, expressionless faces, and extreme lethargy.

The likelihood of panic is high in our culture that is saturated with vampires and zombies in the popular media. The most shocking feature is hemorrhage, usually from multiple areas such as the eyes, ears, gums, nose, rectum and vagina and even spontaneous and unstoppable hemorrhage from needle sticks or small skin tearing injuries. The blood is highly infectious. Late disease becomes severe with sustained extraordinarily high fever, confusion, irritability, and aggression, and finally death from severe blood loss and shock.

"Diagnosis can only be made in a very few special laboratories. For this potential super epidemic, our mobile labs are equipped to deal with the question in an individual on site. To make a definitive diagnosis, we must employ:

- Electron or other very high magnification—up to 100,000 times—with negative stain technology to identify the characteristic "Shephard's crook" filamentous pathogens.
- ELISA [enzyme-linked immunosorbent assay]

- Antigen detection tests
- Serum neutralization test;
- RT-PCR [Reverse-transcriptase polymerase chain reaction assay]
- Virus isolation in cell culture.

"Treatment is palliative, and not often successful. Severe cases require intensive supportive care, especially with IV fluid replacement. An epidemic of any sizable proportion would rapidly overwhelm our doctors' offices, ERs, and hospitals. Prevention is absolutely crucial.

"Prevention must include quarantine, with draconian severity if necessary. Pets, especially monkeys, must be kept indoors and away from humans who have been exposed. Pigs which get infected amplify the disease and must be protected, even placed inside buildings, to protect them from bats. Secretions, blood, urine, and feces must be handled with hazmat level care.

Reducing the rate and magnitude of development of an epidemic in humans will likely require widespread media coverage. I, for one, am glad to see Dr. Norcroft, from Wolf News, here. We at the CDC have concluded that every bit of truthful media coverage and education will be beneficial to curtail the spread, even if panic develops. We are talking about human infection and death, possibly on a very large scale. It will take every resource of the health-care system and law enforcement capability to save us if we cannot find and destroy the vials of virus that we think are out there."

Special Agent Nichols looked over at Sybil, "Well, Dr. Norcroft, you—the clinician, the media hero, and the fighter—have center stage."

Sybil laughed, "I'll have to accept some of that. I agree with Dr. Thomas's assessment and recommendations. May I suggest that we get Dr. Patel and WWN involved right away and give feeds to all of the channels, radio stations, newspapers, etc. That is a political and governmental responsibility. In the background, our action team can work to find hosts and their terrorist plans.

"I am afraid that we should be looking for infected individuals moving around in our society intentionally sticking needles in the unsuspecting. It is possible for a weaponized virus to be aerosolized and spread by what appears to be an innocuous spray—one perhaps containing perfume or a cooling additive—which might not alarm a victim. Large gatherings—even our political and governing institutions, churches, entertainment venues, etc.—would be perfect soft targets for determined terrorists, even ones who are not infected, as in the case of an aerosol vector. We will have to begin to accumulate what we need to treat the severely infected, starting today, I think."

Dr. Thomas turned to Sybil, "Dr. Norcroft, you already have a huge audience. I'll get you all of the pictorial help we have at the CDC, and I suggest you leave here and give one of those 'Breaking News' features within the hour. We all need to be prepared for the fall-out."

Sybil took Dr. Thomas's thumb-drive collection and raced to the airport where the FBI had arranged for a quick helicopter flight to the main headquarters of Wolf News. In half an hour, Greg Nathanson, the morning anchor, was announcing "Breaking News from our medical consultant, Dr. Sybil Norcroft."

Chapter Five

S ybil's broadcast sky-rocketed her fame the minute it was
aired, and held it in the top spot for the five days of the
repetitious news cycle. Her initiation into the world of the
famous and easily recognized was almost instant and complete. For the next five days, her programs, panel presen-
tations, question and answer sessions, and debates were on
television eight to ten times every day. She still had not had
her welcoming in-depth prime time interview with Barbara
Welhelme, but it was being touted almost hourly by the
Wolf channel.

During her time away from the studios, Sybil went on
minor investigative forays with Special Agent Zacharia
Nichols, and sometimes with CIA Agent Edgar Simonsen,
and less often with both of them and CDC teams. For a
week, their efforts were futile. Then, a bit of serendipity
resulted in their first break.

Charles Daniels arranged with his now increasingly popular and in-demand wife to go to the Capitol Building for
a congressional hearing of the Agriculture Department's

activities centered on the department's generous practices of sharing American agricultural know-how with less developed countries. The minority Tea Party members were lodging complaints that the majority Democrats in both houses were giving away U.S. secrets and wasting taxpayers' money in the process. Charles was asked to be a witness about such practices from the perspective of a major global agri-business leader.

The meeting was scheduled for eleven o-clock, and Sybil and Charles were walking up towards the entrance to the House of Representatives which served to admit only persons with official business. Charles was carrying on a discussion with Sybil about the issues he was going to discuss and was practicing what he was going to say, when he looked to his right at the line of tourists waiting to enter the House for a tour.

"Sybil," he said, "do you see that guy standing in the middle of the line—grey jacket, wool knit cap?"

"Um hmmh," she said, not very interested.

"He looks like he's in a Halloween costume—like a zombie. I swear, it looks so real, and so inappropriate. Look."

Some little inkling niggled at her in the back of her brain. Her attention became full when the young woman in front of him jumped away and began rubbing her arm. She looked at it and at him, but apparently decided that nothing had really happened. But, for Sybil, something did happen. She had a moment of bright clarity.

"Charles, I'm so sorry, but I have to go after that guy. That's not a Halloween costume; that's the real thing. He is in shock, and I think he just stuck the girl in front of him with a needle. Did you see her jump?"

"Come to think of it, I did. I'll call the Capitol police, and you go after him; but don't let him touch you. I believe everything you say on TV. You be careful."

They both got on their mobile phones—Charles to the police, and Sybil to Zacharia Nichols.

"Zach, this is Sybil. I think I just caught a break. I am at the Capitol Building, and I am looking at a zombie. In fact, as I get closer, I can see some blood on his pants and dripping out of his sleeve. I think he just stuck a young woman in front of him with a needle."

"Don't do anything until I get there. I'm on my way."

"That's not a good idea. In a few minutes, he'll be inside the House tourist areas with free reign to infect everyone he contacts. I have to stop that. I'll get my husband to help if the Capitol police don't get here in time. See you."

She ran down the short decline towards the line of tourists. Running at the Capitol is a signal to the security forces much like that of scampering prey to a leopard. A cop appeared out of nowhere and intersected Sybil. Charles moved swiftly up behind them.

"Ma'am, what's the rush? What's going on?"

"Officer, I'm Dr. Sybil Norcroft. You may have seen me on TV. I am working with the FBI task force on the Marburg virus terrorism thing. I just saw a man that I think is involved. We have to get to him before he enters the building. Please don't interfere, but, instead help me. This is my husband. All three of us are needed."

"Pretty far-fetched, you have to admit," the police officer said.

"Call Special Agent Zacharia Nichols. Here, I have him on my speed dial. Please hurry, the guy has only two people ahead of him before he gets through the door."

The officer had a vague recollection of having seen Sybil on the tube during the last three days. He made a quick decision and started to move in the direction of the door to the House. He had Sybil's cell phone in his hand and was listening to the dial tones as he moved.

"The guy that looks like a zombie?" he asked Charles and Sybil as they began to hurry the last few steps.

"That's the one. Take him down, but watch out. I think he has an infected needle. Don't let any of that blood get on you."

Zacharia answered and gave the officer a curt "okay" to go ahead. There was no time to waste.

The officer and Charles roughly moved the zombie out of the line and took him to the ground exercising every precaution. Sybil ran past the guard at the door and grabbed the young woman and pulled her out of the line and back outside. The guard—presuming that he was dealing with some kind of a violent criminal—moved to grab Sybil.

The other police officer shouted, "No. Lester, she's with me. Do what she says."

Sybil said to the young woman, "Sit here on the sidewalk. I'll explain in a minute."

The twenty-something year old girl looked shocked and afraid but did as she was told.

"Stop that line and bring out the next five people who were ahead of the zombie guy. Have them sit here by this nice young woman," Sybil ordered.

The next man in line said, "I know who you are. You're the doctor on Wolf who is working with the feds to prevent the Ebola epidemic."

"Marburg, to be precise; but yes, that's me."

"Hey, I didn't think anything of it at the time, but I'm pretty sure the guy stuck me with a needle."

He rolled up his sleeve and showed Sybil a tiny puncture wound.

"I'm sure you're right. That's a big help. Please sit here with these other people. I'll explain in a minute."

Everything seemed to be under control as Zach and his team raced up to where the activity was taking place. They all had hazmat clothes on.

Charles said, "I only touched the clothes on his back. No blood or anything. Think it would be all right if I got to my meeting?"

Sybil looked at Zach who nodded his okay.

"Yes. Take off. I'll see you for dinner tonight if this thing doesn't escalate."

The CDC hazmat team arrived and took over. They created a cordon sanitaire around the area and took all of the seated people into a tent that seemed to have come from nowhere. The bewildered citizens had showers with antibiotic soap, and the two people who were stuck with a needle were detained for questioning and quarantine.

The questioning yielded nothing of value except that they had not seen anyone else who looked like a zombie, nor had they had any idea that anyone else had been stuck by a needle. The two who had been stuck were dismayed and frightened. They were whisked away peremptorily to the CDC hospital wing set up in advance at the NIH [National Institutes of Health] for what would turn out to be a very long stay. Both got infected and the man subsequently died.

On the other hand, questioning the zombie was fruitful. He and his wife had been sitting with their three-year-old daughter when they were subjected to a home invasion. Both of them were given IV injections and forced to stay in their house until they became symptomatic. Then, they were given a small vial of a clear viscous liquid and told to go out and prick people with the fine needles they were given. The wife had been ordered to go around a large shopping mall, and the husband to get into the House of Representatives tour and puncture as many people as they could. Their daughter was held hostage; so, they would not betray the hostage takers.

"What do the men look like who invaded your home?" Sybil asked as a CDC team was dispatched to pick up his wife, and a SWAT team was sent to save the little girl.

"Am I going to die?" he asked. "I am so sick. I feel like I'm going to die."

"I don't know for sure," Sybil said, "but we will do everything in our power to save you and your wife. Now give me a description, please."

One of the FBI special agents came forward with a sketch pad and made drawings of the two men as the unfortunate zombie-appearing victim struggled to focus and to help."

"You did good," Sybil praised him.

He did not look good. His skin was becoming progressively more grey by the minute. It was obvious that he did not have long to live and was miserable. He was going into shock, and there was no vaccine or known anti-infective agent available. Sybil and Zach decided that they were not going to get anything more useful from the poor man; so, they turned him over to the CDC hazmat team who took him to the NIH to join his wife. Their little girl was examined and pronounced to be fine by the CDC doctor and taken to relatives for keeping. Her mother and father were dead two days later.

Every available federal, state, and local agency put out the sketches to their constituency to find out if anyone could give the task force a lead as to where they had come from and especially if anyone had seen the boxes containing the vials, and possibly the antidote.

There was nothing more to do; so, Sybil returned to the Wolf studios and gave a filmed interview which led the next hour's segment as another exclusive Breaking News feature. Charles's interview went well; Sybil was finished in time to get back to Georgetown to pick Cerisse up from the Georgetown Visitation Preparatory School; and they all met up for dinner. In what was to become a hard-and-fast family tradition everyone told everyone else what their day's adventures had been. On this first evening of the tradition, Charles and Sybil concentrated on their happy little girl's experiences at the school. She had brought a letter from the headmistress with her, and everything was very positive. It had been a good day all around.

The task force began to sift through the 1136 call-in reports from the Washington D.C. area which indicated a sighting of the two men in the sketches of the home invaders who infected Peter and Marina Henline. Of these, 842 proved to be valid but led nowhere. The task did not have an address, a name, a workplace, a history—nothing. 92 confessions proved to be spurious, almost entirely from habitual confessors, most of whom were mentally ill. The remaining 202 yielded temporary promise, but after a week of intensive investigation, the information—while probably accurate—did not go anywhere. There was progress. It came from the CDC. The disease control center received 68 reports from physicians that were validated. All of the 68 tested positive and were becoming sick. Every one of them came from the D.C. area which was something of a relief that the infection had not spread beyond the boundaries of the capital city. Agent Simonsen's work abroad did not turn up any cases.

Sybil had nothing to contribute for the time being; so, she and Charles began working on the formal adoption process to make Cerisse their legal daughter and a citizen of the United States. The latter was simple. It took no more than a letter with photos and videos attached to convince the State Department that it was profoundly unsafe for her to return to the place of her birth. The adoption process was put into motion in an atmosphere of considerable promise.

The next break came on the tenth day of the task force's existence. A beat cop in the District's Edgewood neighborhood was called to an abandoned warehouse after shots were reportedly fired. The building was surrounded by barbed-wire fences with multiple openings cut in the heavy wire mesh. The building was literally covered with drug and gang graffiti. Visible just across the street were a bustling shopping center and new luxury apartments. Officer Kleindinst pushed through one of the openings in the fence and walked to the old warehouse with his gun drawn. He announced that he was from the DCPD, and, receiving no answer, moved into the semi-darkness of the huge building. There was only one large, almost empty floor. In the far corner, he heard low-moaning from several voices punctuated by coughing. He moved to the area of the sounds and flashed his light.

Lying on filthy blood soaked mattresses on the floor or on the unpadded concrete were eleven nearly dead women. They had large bleeding sores and a nearly confluent rash on every portion of exposed skin. There complexions were grey and waxen. Many were bleeding from every bodily orifice, and they moaned in pain. Officer Kleindinst backpedaled rapidly and reported in to the precinct and asked for the

FBI task force and the hazmat team from the CDC to rush to the location.

The entire task force gathered at the site within an hour. The CDC team cleaned them up, started IVs, and made the suffering women as comfortable as possible. Sybil, Edgar, and Zach began questioning them. None of them was so far gone that they could not converse, and the three team mates began to piece together a pattern. They were nurses who had been captured on a tour bus headed to the nation's capital. Their captors subdued them and gave them IV injections before transporting them to shopping malls with small spray canisters. They were extorted by the threat of their captors going after their families. Each evening they were returned to the warehouse where they received some meager rations and water. Each day they watched themselves deteriorate and knew that they had been infected with either Ebola or Marburg.

Vera Martin, RN, MS was the most senior and most lucid of the nurses.

Sybil asked her, "Vera, is there anything you can remember that might help us find these monsters?"

Vera thought hard for a few minutes.

"I don't know if it is worth much, but they talked about having come into the U.S. two weeks ago in groups of three at a time over a two day period. They were speaking French, and they were all very dark black in complexion except for one white man. There were no women. They were all healthy and all wore protective clothing, masks, and gloves. I got a look at the gear when the men left for the evening. The hazmat stuff all came stamped with the name of the supplier. It was called Chateaux du Protection de la Santé, KT4GV-3, Product of France."

"That's great, Vera, we'll get right on it. That can't be a commonly available product," Sybil said.

The resources of the DCPD and FBI kicked into overdrive and found the company in Prince George's County, Maryland that afternoon. It was the only distributor for the French company in the United States. The FBI agents grilled the owners, managers, and employees for an hour and learned the names and addresses of the buyers. Law required authentic and verifiable identification procedures, and that required that the buyers provide real names and addresses. Allowing their victims to see the printing on the hazmat materials was the terrorists' first major mistake.

Sybil made the relevant connection. The names of what she presumed were the black Africans were not the expected tribal names, but rather, Islamic ones—Muhammad, Abdullah, Achmed, Farrukh, and Hassan. The ringer in the mix was Jean-Pierre Alain Pourciau.

"Let's get Edgar to check this guy, Pourciau, in his CIA files. I'll bet a milkshake that he is connected to the Fabrique Pharmaceutique DRC," she said.

And Zach said, "I won't take that bet, but I'll add another one that this is an al Qaeda operation."

"With Fabrique Pharmaceutique DRC working for the jihadists," Sybil said completing their mutual thoughts.

Chapter Six

Sybil left the task force and went to Wolf News and gave another Breaking News feature to be aired on the evening news. She agreed to wait until the task force could follow-up on the new evidence. The FBI, NSA, CIA, DCPD, and NYPD files were tapped, and a treasure trove of information flowed into the hands of the task force. The difficulty was not getting enough information, but was the result of having so much that the combined resources of the agencies and departments was strained.

All of the names they found at the Chateaux du Protection de la Santé Company and another twenty were found to have entered the United States from France within three days of each other; all had been traced to the D.C. and Prince George's County area; and all of them, except Pourciau, had established ties to al Qaeda. Edgar Simonsen left for France to follow-up on the leads with his CIA contacts, and Special Agent Zacharia Nichols and an enhanced FBI SWAT team linked up with their counterparts in the FBI OFO/ SRT [Office of Field Operations-Special Response Team],

Homeland Security OFO/SRT, and STATE [Maryland State Police-Special Tactical Assault Team Element] to approach the cluster of addresses in Prince George's County. Nichols had overall command over the small army of elite law enforcement special forces.

Zach let Sybil know when the action was ready to go, and Wolf News flew her and Evan Crutchfield and Doug Mason, her photographers, to the mission launch site. Everyone was suited up in Kevlar vests and helmets.

Zach took a moment to inform the Wolf News crew what was going to take place, "Look, you guys, this could get very nasty. You are here as a special privilege. Don't abuse it. Stay back until I signal you. I worry about the cops in all of this, and my career is over if any one of you gets wounded or killed. I'll see to it that you get as much information as I am allowed to give you and as soon as I can get it to you. But no scoop is worth any one of your lives. *Capiche?*"

"We *capiche*," Sybil said and gave him a mock salute and a genuine smile.

"I don't want to see a single weapon on any of you, not even a Swiss Army Knife."

"*Jawohl!*" Sybil said crisply.

Another set of shared salutes and smiles, and Zach went back to his troops.

"Load up. Watch each other's backs. Let's get this show on the road."

The Maryland state officers set up a mile square perimeter and patrolled it so closely that not even a rat could escape. They then went systematically door-to-door and evacuated the area to within five blocks of the apartments they presumed were inhabited by the al Qaeda operatives. The FBI and Homeland Security units drove along different streets in MRAPs [heavy armored SWAT-Mine-Resistant Ambush Protected] vehicles and unmarked cars. Zach and his personal team set up the Mobile Command Center. Sybil and her crew were in their own FBI BearCat SWAT armored vehicle parked immediately behind the Mobile Command Vehicle. HRT [FBI Hostage Rescue and Counter-Terrorism Team] helicopters hovered overhead. Communications were established and tested.

Zach checked the readiness of his troops, "Know that this is a high risk arrest situation, and Murphy's Law is in effect. Be careful, be coordinated, no heroes. One last check-in."

Twenty-six separate stations checked in. All was a go.

Zach gave the signal. Elite agents fast-roped from three helicopters as an army of highly trained and skilled emergency officers poured into the streets, each with their own targeted address. Within three minutes the unmistakable sounds of a war commenced. Flash-bangs, automatic rifle fire, and combat shotgun rounds pierced the air. Men's yelling voices added to the controlled chaos of the operation.

As soon as the assault teams proper entered the buildings known to be housing the terrorists, a second phalanx of officers began a systematic evacuation of the adjacent civilians even as the confusion of battle was still underway. That unit of officers was equally as highly trained as the assault teams, and within ten minutes a large group of frightened and cowed citizens were herded into the neighborhood's Harriet Tubman elementary school and put under heavy security guard.

Doug and Evan got great footage of the whole scene, and sent it back digitally to Wolf News even as the action was taking place. Sybil was filmed in the safety of the armored vehicle giving a minute-by-minute account of developments which added further drama to her report. More than 100 million Americans were glued to the Sybil Norcroft Report, as it was now billed. The rapt audience had everything: action, noise, great filming, and a movie-star quality cool and calm reporter who looked as if she had been in such situations for a long career as a battlefield journalist. By the end of the day, one would have had to be stranded on Mars not to be aware of the new star of world news, Sybil Norcroft.

Out in the real world, mopping up operations were underway. Zach and his FBI officers came out of the neighborhood leading more than a dozen dazed and thoroughly humbled terrorist operatives—all Africans—and all ready and eager to talk. None of them needed another object lesson about their incredibly formidable opponent.

By the end of the operation when the crime scene analysis specialists were combing the neighborhood and all of its buildings, it was painfully clear that the principle targets—Jean-Pierre Alain Pourciau and the boxes of biological weapons were not among the captured. There were plenty of Muhammads, Abdullahs, Achmeds, Farrukhs, and Hassans; and they were questioned for the next 30 hours until every tidbit of information was wrung out of them. Zach told Sybil that he would get her as much information as they could collate and print and that was not classified by the following morning.

When she got home in Georgetown, Charles and Cerisse greeted her with bear hugs.

"And, how was your day, wifey?" Charles asked innocently.

They laughed, and Sybil regaled her husband and daughter with exciting tales until the wee hours of the night.

Wolf News ran rehashes and commentaries on the activities of the previous day while they waited for more news-worthy material to come in from the FBI. Sybil was on in person three times during the day, but it was slow; and she was able to get away early. That was important to her because. Dr. Stephanie Bradshaw, headmistress of her daughters school—prospective school—had been after her to come and have a talk about Cerisse's needs and future.

Sybil drove from home with Cerisse to the school. Dr. Bradshaw approved of the little girl being able to hear what was said between the adults interested in her welfare.

"Well, Dr. Norcroft, you've become quite the celebrity of late. I have been following your reports every day; they are fascinating and chilling, I must say."

"It has been like something between a rodeo and a circus— the old saw, 'never-a-dull-moment', is a huge understatement of my life since I got to Wolf News. Whoda thunk? Thanks for being patient with me. I do care about your concerns, and I am certainly fully invested in Cerisse. For your information, most of the formal adoption process is behind us."

"That's wonderful news. Let me give you some more, but mine is tempered with a 'but' or two."

"You have my full attention."

"All of this past week or ten days must seem like being in a whirlwind to Cerisse. She is in a new country, trying to learn a new language, going to school on a regular basis for the first time, adjusting to a new family—the only real and functional family she has ever known for that matter. As near as anyone can tell, Cerisse is 14-years-old and going on 30 in terms of her life's experience. Her sexual experience—as horrible as it was—is planets beyond the other girls in the school. They listen to her tell of her life with jaws hanging open. We will hardly need a sex-education class in the school if she continues to regale our girls with life on the seamy side. Don't get me wrong; I am not a prude; but our girls are not ready for her; and she is not ready for them. You have an extremely valuable opportunity to do something about sex trafficking, Dr. Norcroft. I hope you can run with stories on that subject when the Marburg virus episode comes to a close."

"That's an idea I'll tuck into the back of my brain for a while, but I think you are right. But, for now, are you telling me that you can't or won't let her attend your school?"

"It probably sounds like I'm saying that, but that's not exactly the case. I have a proposition and a few suggestions I would like you to consider."

"Anything that will help Cerisse."

"She needs to see a psychologist, one who specializes in dealing with highly sexualized children, maltreated children, and underprivileged children. Cerisse is all of that. Secondly, she needs to have an intensive immersion in English as a second language. I know you speak French fluently, and I think Charles needs to get a Rosetta Stone course and at least get the rudiments. However, that said, she must fight her way through the confusing and difficult English language; so, she can succeed in society and in school. You need to avoid speaking French with her as much as is practically possible. Finally, she needs to have a full physical and lab examination. Children with her background regularly have parasites, Tb, recurrent malaria, and, difficult as it is for me to bring up; she could easily have an STD."

Sybil's famous calm and ice-bloodedness served her well. She did not flinch at any of the suggestions.

"Charles and I will get started tomorrow. Even with all of those changes accomplished, how can you teach her, since she is almost at a kindergarten level in her education instead of at the eighth grade where she should be?"

"The school and the family can split the costs of special tutors, special cultural immersions; and we can move her along towards grade level over something like two years. It'll take work and patience. Think your new-found stardom and responsibilities will leave you enough time for the Cerisse project?"

Dr. Bradshaw's facial expression portrayed her serious concerns as much as did what she had to say.

"I will make it happen. Like you, Dr. Bradshaw, I have had to overcome some considerable obstacles to get where I am. I don't suppose I am any genius, but I am a worker. I will find time. Charles and I will make sacrifices. We will prevail. Help us and grant us some slack as we get started, all right?"

"That is exactly the spirit I wanted to get from you. Consider us partners. I am Stephanie, would it be all right if I call you Sybil?"

"Yes, Stephanie—partner. We have a deal."

Special Agent Zacharia Nichols called Sybil at her Wolf News office three days later.

"Hi, Zach, what's up?" Nichol asked after Zach said hello.

"We have a good lead on Jean-Pierre Alain Pourciau; just how good, time will tell. I think we have something of a trail that may need a good clinician to follow. Do you have some time today?"

"I do. It's a slow news day for me. I need to get out and earn my keep."

"I'll pick you up in an hour. Wear scruffies."

Sybil had learned to keep a set of her combat clothes in her office, including Kevlar vest and helmet, her Glock .30, and her K-bar knife. She was always ready.

"I'll be in the main lobby," she said.

Zach and two other special agents arrived in 55 minutes.

"You must have been toilet trained too early," Sybil joked.

"It's the FBI training," he said; and they smiled at each other, having established a trusting and comfortable working relationship.

They drove to the FBI helicopter airport and flew to Loudoun County, Virginia, just outside of Leesburg. On the way, Zach told her that they had a couple of bodies. Local law enforcement had gotten a tip that some very sick black people and a big military looking white man were seen entering a small cabin by Banshee Reeks Nature Preserve where no one was supposed to be after eight in the evening. When the officers investigated, they found the remains of two men who could not have been dead for more than a few hours. The officers thought that their having come by spooked the white man, and he left without taking all of his belongings.

The cabin was cordoned off with yellow tape and was under analysis by the county CSI unit.

"I'm Zach Nichols, and this is Dr. Sybil Norcroft. We don't want to interfere, but we are already deeply involved in the case. We'd appreciate it if you would bring us up to speed."

"You taking over?" the lead detective said with an expectant frown.

"Nothing like that. We need anything we can get here and to move on to wherever the evidence points us."

"Well, that's refreshing," the detective said. "Here's what we know to this point."

They got a succinct rendition of what was known and what was found. The bodies showed evidence of stab wounds, and a skin rash. It was an obvious double murder. There were some maps of D.C. and two throwaway cell phones, one of which was smashed beyond repair. The other had been found by the Loudoun County detectives under a pile of trash in what passed for a makeshift kitchen.

"No boxes with Marburg containing vials or antidotes, I take it?"

"Sorry, we thought of that and searched all over the place and outside. *Nada.*"

Zach turned the phone on and went straight to recent messages. He scrolled down the short list.

"All but three of these are to the same number. It's a D.C. prefix. I'll send the contents into the lab, and we'll see what turns up."

He connected the throwaway to his bureau issue cell and thumbed in two or three stokes.

"It's on its way to the lab," he told Sybil.

The other things of interest the detectives found were a discarded bottom of a hazmat suit with a fairly large rip in it and blood on the pant leg and a memo paper written in Arabic and French. Sybil quickly translated the memo:

"Brother in the work of Allah, our targets are easy ones—old and unable to mount a defense. Two planeloads will arrive at Dulles at two in the afternoon and will be bused to the place by an hour, maybe a little more, after that. God is with you. We will hit the decadent Great Satan where it hurts the most with this choice. They will know that none of them are ever safe anywhere. With God's help, our message will spread like the plague in Egypt, and will be unstoppable.

Only we, the men of God, will have the means to protect ourselves. Allahu akhbar!"

Sybil rummaged in the trash on the floor with the end of a broken broom handle. She turned up two items.

"Look at these, Zach. Two $10,000 money wrappers."

"They are certainly well funded. It is pretty unusual for people to use cash in these times of electronic and plastic card money," Zach said. "I get a BOLO out to everybody in the D.C. to be on the lookout for a man or men paying with cash."

"I think we can limit that to the area near the mall, Zach. Everything on the maps and in that memo point to the World War II memorial. The planeloads have to be part of the Honor Flight Network which brings the vets into D.C. every year to see the memorial. I think this tells us that the martial looking white man had to be Jean-Pierre Alain Pourciau, and he is going to be in or around that memorial today at about threeish. He could be alone, or he could have some kind of idiot helpers handling the infliction of the infectious agents," Sybil asserted. "Let's get there."

"Okay, but we have to be in hazmat protective suits. It's too dangerous even to get near that virus."

"It will look like an invasion by space aliens if we do. We are going to have to take our chances and to blend in as well as we can. Maybe we'll run onto some sick people, and we can prevent them from hurting any more people," Sybil said with increasing emphasis.

"I can't ask you to do that, Sybil. The director would have my badge and gun if I did or maybe even large chunks of my hide."

"You're not asking. I'm telling. I'm going. Now, times awastin'."

Zach shrugged in defeat, and they returned to the helicopters to fly back to the FBI heliport. They were met by six black Suburbans filled with men and women in everyday clothes. At least they did not have blue windbreakers with large gold letters on the back heralding the fact that they were FBI. By the same reasoning, the brave souls were not wearing any hazmat protection. A mildly astute criminal observer would tumble to the fact that they were law enforcement officers, but at least it was not flagrant.

The officers came in from all entrances to the mall and made every effort to blend in and to look the part of lookyloo tourists. Sybil, Doug, and Evan entered on the sidewalk between the Lincoln and Korean War memorials. She walked along the edge of the reflection pool towards the center of the mall where the World War II memorial stood. There was a large crowd of spectators, politicians, old vets and their wheelchair attendants, and media personnel. The Mall was busy but calm. The law enforcement officers and their temporary partners from Wolf News scanned the crowds milling about. Sybil decided to concentrate on the WWII vets. After looking for five or ten minutes, she had another moment of serendipity.

Chapter Seven

She had been looking but not seeing, at least not getting her brain involved. Most of the veterans were in wheel chairs being pushed by neatly dressed young men and occasionally by a young woman. The attendants were hands-on, always pushing the chair or leaning forward to speak to their patient or stopping to adjust an IV line or to prevent the IV pole from toppling over as uneven lawn was encountered. Now that Sybil was fully engaged, she became aware that milling around among the veterans were about ten, maybe twelve, men who never seemed to be helping or talking to anyone. The attendants and the veterans were ignoring those men for the most part.

The clincher for Sybil came when she realized that the interlopers were holding small spray bottles and from time to time pausing to spray a mist into the face of the veteran they were near or at the attendant or both. The vets and their attendants all seemed to be good-natured about the minor annoyance. After all, it was hot, and the mist must not have had an unpleasant taste or odor and apparently did not burn the recipient's eyes.

Sybil almost cried aloud—"stop, that is the Marburg virus. You're being infected!" but she controlled herself and looked around frantically for a police officer or an FBI agent. She could not be sure of any of them. She tried to see Zach. He came into view, but he was on the opposite side of the Mall and just then entering the WWII memorial itself. It would be futile to shout. Doug and Evan were by her side.

"You guys take a good look at that bunch of old vets. See the men mingling around them."

"Yeah," Doug said, not fully comprehending the significance of Sybil's comment at first.

Evan got it, "There spritzing mist into everybody's faces over there. That has to be the Marburg aerosol. Where're all of the cops? We gotta do something."

Sybil said, "Take pictures and follow me. Tell me if you see anybody you know that is in law enforcement. We'll see what we can do!"

They were sprinting now.

"Stop that! Stop spraying that mist into people's faces! Everybody…that's the deadly virus you have been hearing about on TV. Don't let them spray you. Get away!"

By now, the crowd was beginning to make sense of what she was saying.

A young man rushed up to her and said, "Hey, you're on Wolf. You're the health reporter…Dr. Norcroft, right?"

"Yes," she said and rushed on.

He persisted, "How about an autograph. Do you charge for signing one?"

Sybil started to get angry with the young man, but instead cooled down; and still running, said to him, "Help us. Tackle every one of the guys that are spraying our veterans. They're killing them."

That was all the young man needed. He hit one after the other of the sprayers and bowled them over like a defensive linebacker.

"Don't touch them or let them spray you. Watch out for needles," Sybil called to him.

He nodded. Another couple of young stalwarts caught on to what was happening and came to his assistance.

The ensuing commotion attracted law enforcement. The legitimate attendants were now actively moving their venerable old charges out of harm's way, knowing that—for many of them—it was too late. They had already been exposed. A park policeman pulled his 9 mm and aimed it at one of the sprayers.

"Halt. Police. Drop the sprayer! Now!"

The sprayer pulled a handgun and fired off two rounds before the young police officer could defend himself. He died almost before he hit the ground. The sprayer turned towards Sybil and got off one round before the wheel-chair confined octogenarian beside him swung his cane around and cracked the man in the face. The sprayer cried out and clasped his broken nose. He dropped both of his weapons and turned to run.

A second policeman shot him in the head. There was now a small army of law enforcement officers who were aiding the vets and their helpers, rounding up the terrorists and separating them from the innocents, and calling the CDC hazmat teams. In minutes that area of the National Mall became a crime scene, a murder investigation site, and a quarantine center. The vets and their attendants who had been sprayed were given clothes-on showers with antibiotic soap. EMTs began systematically putting drops of antibiotics suspended in saline into every person's eyes that came within an arm's length of the EMT.

Sybil caught up with the young man who had been so helpful and expressed her gratitude.

"Let me help some more. This is exciting stuff, but I can keep my cool. You need protection."

Sybil knew he was probably right; so, she agreed. She turned and began running towards where she had last seen Zach Nichols. When she was less than fifty yards away from that spot, she caught sight of the tall athletic blond man she recognized as Jean-Pierre Alain Pourciau. On the opposite side of the memorial, she saw Zach in her peripheral vision.

Almost as she said it, she knew it was a mistake, "Zach, it's him. Look this way!"

The FBI special agent turned in Sybil's direction and found himself looking into Pourciau's soulless eyes. They were less than ten yards apart. Zach hesitated for a fraction of a second to avoid hurting a bystander. Pourciau had no such scruples—he had no scruples. He knew instinctively that the law enforcement officer was wearing a Kevlar vest; so, he fired at Zach's head. His aim was off by a fraction, and the 9 mm slug hit Zach in the neck just to the left of center. Blood burst in a geyser. Zach dropped his gun and made a futile attempt to staunch the erupting hemorrhage. He fell over dead with a quizzical expression on his face.

Pourciau quickly changed directions and tried to locate Sybil. She was racing towards one of the vertical marble slabs that memorialized a state's contribution to the Second World War. He got off a shot but missed her and killed a bystander, a young mother pushing her twin babies in a baby carriage. The deadly bullet struck her in the chest, and she folded over the handle of the carriage and crumpled to the ground tipping the carriage over on its side. Now, there were police officers everywhere. Evan and Doug were busy capturing the whole chaotic scene for the news channel. They were getting great footage.

Pourciau made a dash for the east exit of the memorial knocking over anyone who got in his way. An elderly veteran, dressed in his marine uniform, deliberately jumped into Pourciau's way knocking him off balance. The agitated terrorist raised his gun and shot the brave veteran twice in the chest before rushing on. Hundreds of cell phone cameras recorded every move that the terrorist and his pursuers made. Many dozens of photos and videos captured Sybil in motion as she tried desperately to get to the killer.

The height of irony for the old veteran was that he had survived five years of war, having been in almost every major campaign in the war in Europe. He saw months and months of combat and never even got a Purple Heart. He died a violent death in the safety of the memorial to him and his comrades-in-arms' service.

Pourciau fired off an occasional wild round at Sybil and missed her every time. He wounded two more innocent bystanders and a veteran FBI agent. Sybil, her two cameramen, the young man who had assisted in saving the coterie of wheel chair bound vets, and five law enforcement officers continued the chase as they left the grassy area of the Mall and began heading towards the Capitol Building. All of the pursuers were wary, and it was apparent that the terrorist was slowly outdistancing them. Evan and Doug were gasping for breath. It was hard work to run and shoot, watch out for people in their way, and to try and keep up.

Without warning, Pourciau suddenly stopped, dropped to one knee and took careful aim. He hit Doug in his Kevlar protected chest and knocked him down. He fired again and put a round dead center in Evan's forehead. There was nothing Sybil could do for her co-workers. Doug was already beginning to shake off the stunning blow that had hit and bruised his chest. Evan was dead. Her young admirer took in the situation with full understanding.

"Let's get that monster," he said.

"Get film footage," Sybil said and started to run.

The young man hefted the camera and began to shoot, but Pourciau was now out of sight. The police officers had lost sight of him as well and were dividing up to search in several directions. Police cars, ambulances, helicopters, and SWAT armored vehicles were converging on the area. Capitol police formed a protective shield of men around the government buildings. Everything was carried out in accordance with well-conceived plans by superbly trained officers, and the perpetrator got clean away.

Sybil and her helper returned to where Doug was standing on shaky legs, but otherwise, seemed all right. They all walked over to view Evan's body.

"What a tragedy," Sybil said, "what a terrible waste. Evan Crutchfield was a fine man, too young to die. How awful."

Dean Todd, Sybil's young man, caught every poignant emotion with his camera. He was impressed that the vaunted "Snow Queen" did not shed a tear. Her face betrayed her unyielding anger and hatred. It seemed like a fitting set of emotions to Dean, and later to her now massive world-wide audience.

Sybil desperately wanted to get out of there and to hug her husband and daughter. But first, she had to get Dean to film her as she calmly presented her story to the camera and to the world. Two staffers from the Wolf News network found her and carted away the camera with its precious coverage. Sybil still had to go through an interview with the FBI and Homeland Security with special emphasis on the slain special agent of the FBI. She controlled her emotions to the admiration of her interrogators and to her own surprise. She felt more like a lost and lonely little girl than a battle-hardened combat reporter. It had been a very long day.

Chapter Eight

Ed Simonsen made a contribution to the task force two days later. CIA sources in Montreal had a confirmed sighting of Jean-Pierre Alain Pourciau. Ed forwarded a photo of the international fugitive from his iPhone to the new head of the task force, FBI Special Agent Grant Walsh. Walsh came to the hunt with a burning anger and intense personal involvement. He and Zach Nichols had been classmates at the academy and had remained personal and family friends. The level of search activity increased exponentially with his arrival, and every contact the FBI and CIA had in Canadian law enforcement was contacted. Every old marker was called in. Walsh and his team—which solidly included Sybil—were intensely and personally involved.

Ed said to Sybil, "Look, it's as improbable and as irregular as it can be; but do you want to go with me the French Canada. I like your instincts. I am also convinced that publicity is a major asset in this case and especially in this man-hunt. You and I have been through enough together that you can bring a photographer with you. You up for it?"

Sybil was aware that a real change had taken place in her during the past six weeks. The care and devotion she had lavished on neurosurgery just two months previously, she now had transferred to her new dedication—that of being a serious journalist and media figure.

Without further thought, she impulsively said, "Let's get on with it. I want this guy."

"One rule, Sybil, no pictures of me and no mention of my name or who I work for, okay?"

"Okay."

"You can say that you tried to get the CIA to contribute to your eventual stories, but the CIA would neither confirm nor deny any involvement in the Pourciau case."

Sybil nodded her acquiescence.

She, Doug Mason, her photographer, and Ed Simonsen arrived in YUL [Montréal-Trudeau International Airport] six hours later.

Jean-Pierre Alain Pourciau, traveling under one of his many aliases, had arrived in the cosmopolitan city two days previously having crossed the porous border from the United States in the dark of night and without encountering any U.S. or Canadian customs officials. He was guided by a disgruntled middle-aged New Yorker whose hippie parents had marked out an escape trail for Weatherman fanatics to escape to Canada during the bad years of the 1960s. Pourciau killed his guide when they crossed over through the outskirts of Stanstead, Quebec—a town bisected by the minimally fenced international border line. He was staying in an al Qaeda safehouse—the Algonquin Hotel—in the heart of the city—a seedy remnant of its once proud self. He was keeping a very low profile awaiting a dark-of-night transfer to Iceland and then back to Africa.

After 36 hours, Pourciau got cabin fever. His handlers and hosts warned him ad nauseum to be patient and to keep holed up in the tiny run-down hotel room. Pourciau was having a "nicky-fit." He sneaked out to a Jewish bodega a block from the hotel to get a pack of Du Mauriers. He satisfied his craving by taking his first puffs from two cigarettes at once. That short foray into the outside world was when he was spotted by an attentive off-duty city police officer. The officer happened to be on the payroll of the CIA as a supplement to his meager city cop salary.

Ed had the address of the Algonquin but no information about which room Pourciau was occupying.

He wore an old suit imported from China and sold in all of the Debenham stores, worn but serviceable black crepe soled lace-ups, and a beret. Sybil sported a brunette wig and a baggy dress from a second-hand store that almost concealed her statuesque curves. The photographer, Doug, kept his camera secured under a long soiled double-breasted trench coat. The three of them and Canadian CIA agent, Dirk Ravens, watched the front door of the hotel from the inside of an unmarked off-grey van across the street.

Pourciau and another companion—a swarthy, thick-set, Middle-Eastern looking man in well-seasoned work clothes from Mark's Work Wearhouse—and a lithe athletic appearing woman with short dark hair, dressed in running clothes, got out of an old multi-colored Peugeot in front of the hotel. The vehicle had several unrepaired dents, and the lower third of its body was rust-eaten. The Middle-Eastern bodyguard got out first. His face was a dead giveaway—the face of an over-the-hill pugilist with no neck.

"Heads-up," Ed said unnecessarily.

The CIA agents and Wolf News team waited until the three subjects entered the hotel before they got out of the van. Sybil, Doug, and Dirk went to the left, and Ed went to the right to minimize the chances of being seen by anyone in the Algonquin. The agents peered through the dirty glass door of the even dirtier building and saw Pourciau and his companions turn the corner onto the second floor landing. Doug followed Ed, and they entered the hotel followed closely by Sybil and Dirk. The four of them ran quietly up the first set of stairs. Pourciau and his confederates could be heard walking further on up the creaky stairs.

The terrorists—evidently fully confident that they were safe from prying eyes and ears—made no attempt to be quiet, a good sign to Sybil and the others coming up from below the terrorists that they were as yet undetected.

Pourciau's voice was heard on the fourth floor—one above where the stalkers stood listening.

"Home sweet home," he was saying sarcastically.

"Not for long," the woman's heavily accented Quebecois voice was heard to say.

Ed sprinted silently up the two sets of stairs in time to see the last of the three terrorists enter the fourth door on the right. He moved close enough to the door to get its number, then returned to where Sybil, Dirk, and Doug were standing.

"Let's give them a little time to get settled and maybe have a drink or two and then go in hard. Sybil, I want you and Doug to stay well outside the door. This is going to get nasty unless I miss my bet."

"You are not going to leave me out of this, Ed. I've paid my dues."

"Keep back enough not to get shot, Doc. You're too valuable."

All four of them were wearing Kevlar vests.

Ed and Dirk stood on opposite sides of the door. Ed counted down silently from five on his fingers. As soon as his pinky finger raised, Dirk kicked in the door; and he and Ed rushed in, guns drawn.

"Police!!" Dirk shouted.

The Middle-Eastern thug reached for his gun which was sitting on the kitchen table in front of him and died for his effort. Dirk fired a single round from his sound muffled 9 mm which struck the terrorist just to the left of the center of his forehead.

Doug caught all of the action on his video-cam through the open door. Sybil stood immediately behind him.

Pourciau vaulted across the bed and started climbing out of the window and onto the fire escape landing as soon as Ed stepped into the bedroom. Pourciau nervously fired one shot narrowly missing Ed who back pedaled quickly. He and Dirk did judo rolls into the room concentrating on foiling Pourciau's escape.

They each fired two silenced rounds that missed. Their attention was focused on Pourciau, and they did not see the woman step out of the bathroom to their left. She began firing a stream of bullets from her MP5 machine pistol. One round grazed Ed's shoulder; another two hit Dirk in his head and neck; and a stray round passed through the paper-thin bedroom wall and made a painful through-and-through channel in Sybil's unprotected shoulder. She dropped to the ground more out of surprise than from any deadly effect. Doug got all of the action on his digital camera then called out to Sybil.

"You okay, boss?"

"Hurts like the devil, but I'm okay," she managed.

His quick assessment of her wound confirmed Sybil's own judgment; so, Doug stepped into the bedroom to get good footage of Ed's extended hand firing three rounds into the female terrorist's chest. Lacking a protective vest, she dropped like a rag doll with its stuffing suddenly removed. As soon as she was safely put down, Doug raced to the window to get a few quick images of Pourciau descending the last few rungs of the fire escape ladder and racing away from the building.

Ed called to Dirk, but he knew it was too late to get Pourciau. They had missed him again. It was only then that Ed realized that Dirk was dead; he would get a black star on the entry wall of the CIA building in Langley. He cursed himself for the failure of the mission, for the death of his fellow-agent for whom he had been in charge, and for having been stupid enough to let the high-profile media heroine come along—and worse—to get wounded.

Doug loosely wrapped a bathroom towel around Sybil's shoulder while Ed removed all traces of his and Dirk's CIA involvement.

When he was satisfied, Ed said, "We have to get out of here right now. You up to a brisk walk, Doc?"

Sybil's color had returned, and she said, "I'm okay. It hurts, but I'm pretty sure I can walk or even run. My adrenaline is still pumping, and I seem to be over the initial shock of the gunshot. The worst thing is that I am having real difficulty moving my shoulder. I think that will pass with time; but, for now, I'll be kind of awkward."

Her biggest concern was what was she going to tell Charles and Cerisse when she got home.

Chapter Nine

Charles—along with most of the rest of the country—
had already seen Wolf's report on Sybil's foray into
Canada although the channel left out all information about
the specific location. The dramatic quality of Doug's video
was every bit on a par with anything Raza Patel had ever
done for WWN. However, the footage showing Sybil taking
a bullet eclipsed anything the WWN senior medical consultant had ever had the courage to show. There had been considerable debate among the Wolf editors about whether to
include it, but Sybil had insisted that they should take a little
risk and push the envelope on main channel TV coverage.

The conversation between Charles and Sybil did not go as
well. Her explanation about what she had done was stilted by
his poorly contained anger.

"Sybil, we don't need the money from your work at Wolf,
and we certainly don't need the drama or the grief. Have you
given any real thought about the consequences…aside from
your soaring ratings?"

That comment just slipped out and was meant to hurt in something of the way he was hurting. As soon as he uttered the words, Charles knew that he had disrespected his wife and her integrity, but he could not rein himself in.

"And, any thought about Cerisse? The consequences for her? I can't let her watch TV. You are on everywhere and all of the time."

Sybil waited until the hurricane spent its energy before replying.

"I am genuinely sorry, Charles. I am not a publicity hound as you seem to imply—and that hurts me—but all of it goes along with the job. I will admit that I am now in my real element. I always thought that doing a major intracranial operation made me feel alive, but it was nothing quite like what has been going on since I walked in the door of Wolf News. I'm sorry you had to worry, but it would be disingenuous of me to tell you that I don't like what I do or that it's just a job. I used to have a secret little thrill when I heard a positive comment about how intelligent neurosurgeons are…you know, 'well's it's not brain surgery, but…' until I learned that the smartest people in the world are really New York cab drivers.

"As for Cerisse…and you for that matter, I did worry; and I did care. I still do, of course. I will try my best to be safer, but there are still risks I have to take. I have become one of the sheep dogs William J. Bennett talked about in his speech at the Naval Academy who are up in the night; so, the regular people—the sheep—can be safe in their beds. Please support me. What I'm involved in is bigger than me or us."

"Not for me, Sybil" Charles said. "There is nothing bigger than us. I include Cerisse in 'us'. We love you. Try to understand that."

Sybil wanted to hide her eyes from his. She had expected no less of a confrontation with her long-suffering husband, but it still hurt worse than the lingering pain in her wounded shoulder.

After, Sybil went to shower for bed, Charles looked up the quote by William Bennett on line.

"William J. Bennett said in a lecture to the United States Naval Academy on November 24, 1997 that one Vietnam veteran, an old retired colonel, once said, 'Most of the people in our society are sheep. They are kind, gentle, productive creatures who can only hurt one another by accident or under extreme provocation—the regular people in society who go about their lives unaware of those who protect them or what they do. 'Then there are the wolves,' the old war veteran was quoted as saying, 'the criminals, foreign enemies, and terrorists; and the wolves feed on the sheep without mercy. There are evil men in this world, and they are capable of evil deeds. The moment you forget that or pretend it is not so, you become a sheep. There is no safety in denial.'

"Then there are sheepdogs," Bennett went on, "I'm a sheepdog. I live to protect the flock and confront the wolf." Bennett told the midshipmen about a sign in one California law enforcement agency, 'We intimidate those who intimidate others.'"

Charles was afraid to admit his suspicion, but it appeared that his "delicate flower" of a wife was, in fact, becoming one of the sheep dogs.

Sybil Norcroft, M.D., Ph.D., F.A.C.S. and her intrepid news photographer, Doug Mason, were the heroes and stars of the week. However, the news anchors and the public wanted to spin it when they returned to the studio to work. Sybil and Doug both gave three interviews on the action-packed hunt for the Marburg terrorists. Each of them gave a heartfelt eulogy for their lost comrade-in-arms, Evan Crutchfield, and made an oblique references to the law enforcement and "other" officers who had fallen in this latest battle against al Qaeda jihadist terrorism. Those interviews and Doug's great video footage carried them for the rest of the week.

Sybil used the extra time to go to one of the CDC's field station treatment centers where she suited up in hazmat gear and plunged into the work of trying to save as many of the several thousands of surviving victims of Pourciau and the al Qaeda monsters who pulled his strings. As they doggedly worked on the victims, no one involved could let go of the hatred they harbored for the man and his diabolical use of a biological weapon of mass destruction on innocents.

She was comfortable in the anonymity of her yellow hazmat suit and honed and strengthened her skills for treating shock, which—along with hemorrhage—was the major cause of death for the Marburg victims. The fatality rate was dreadful and extremely discouraging to the doctors, nurses, and the rest of the all-volunteer staff. The occasional save had to be its own reward. Doug got good candid footage of Sybil at work and a couple of face-time interviews which he kept sending back to Wolf to keep the story alive. Sybil felt self-conscious about being in the limelight so prominently, but knew that this was all what she had signed on to do.

Three days later, Special Agent Grant Walsh, head of the combined task force, called Sybil on her cell phone.

"Doctor Norcroft, we have some information on Jean-Pierre Pourciau's whereabouts and are going to go after him. Or, I should say that our CIA friends in the person of your working partner, Ed Simonsen, are working a plan. He asked me to see if you could attend a meeting at FBI headquarters tomorrow morning at nine."

"Sure, I'll be there. What have you found out?"

"Not on the phone."

"Of course. See you in the a.m."

Walsh presented the evidence.

"We have travel records. Pourciau and his aliases made a convoluted trip from Montreal to Reykjavík and on to Kinshasa. This is what we have:"

He put the information from the international airport watch lists and the international BOLO on the conference room's screen.

8-17-13 SUBJECT passport scan for Alphonse Trudeau, Canadian citizen on the watch list at YMX, Montréal–Mirabel International Airport, at 22:03 hrs, 08-16-13. Security check and search. Questioned by Customs Agent DuParrier, see transcript #13-24891. Released 22:36 hrs. Departed Montréal for REK [Reykjavík International Airport] on Lufthansa Flight 1769 at 23:21 hrs.

8-19-13 SUBJECT passport scan for Drakan Holterman, Qatar citizen on the watch list at REK [Reykjavík International Airport] at 04:46 hrs, 08-18-13. Security check and search. Questioned by Customs Agent Thorkeldsson, see transcript #13-89774. Released 06:51 hrs. Departed Reykjavik for KRT [Khartoum International Airport], at 10:30 hrs on Emirates Airlines, Flight 473.

8-23-13 SUBJECT passport scan for Heinrich Schinklemann, German citizen on the watch list at KRT [Khartoum International Airport] at 18:52 hrs, 08-18-13. Security check and search. Questioned by Security Agent Siddig, see transcript #13-18882. Released 19:24 hrs.

Departed Khartoum for JUB [International Airport, Juba, South Sudan] at 21:20 hrs on Ethiopian Airlines, Flight 305.

8-31-13 SUBJECT passport scan for Jean-Pierre Alain Pourciau performed but SUBJECT not detained, searched, or questioned. Routine record search by FBI special agents with permission by security forces at FIH [Ndjili International Airport, Kinshasa, DRC] performed six days after SUBJECT's arrival on 8-25-13. Records show arrival by Egyptair, but this cannot be verified. See transcript #13-09176.

BOLO
[Interagency Fugitive Notice]

MESSAGE BEGINS
Message Origin: United States Department of Justice
Date and time of Transmission: 13, August, 2013, 0921
Message Recipients: Lead and Communications responsibility—IFO (Interagency Fugitive Operations); USMS (All 94 offices), FBI, ATF, DEA, JTF-6, NCIC, VICAP, FLO, NYPD FAT SQUAD, INS, CIA, NSC, ALL STATE AND D.C. POLICE AND MAJOR CITY POLICE OFFICES, ALL FPUs and STATE PURSUIT UNITS.
Canada: CPIC, FIRS-Nationwide.
U.K.: Scotland Yard, U.K. wide Special Police Forces, SOCA-Serious Organized Crime Agency,
France: Gendarmerie National, Police Nationale
Russia: Federal Security Service (FSB), Ministry of Internal Affairs Militsiya, OMON: Russian—Отряд милиции особого назначения; Otryad Militsii Osobogo Naznacheniya, Special Purpose Police Unit (ОМОН)
Interpol

Subject:
Jean-Pierre Alain Pourciau.

Criminal Status:
International terrorists with direct links with jihadist terrorist
list organization, al Qaeda. Unlawful acts including class A
felony murder, murder (2 counts of a law enforcement officer),
mass murder with a WMD—biological agent, assault, inter-
state and international transportation of firearms and use of
firearms against law enforcement officers, forgery and false use
of a passport, fraud, misuse of visas and other identification
documents, false personation, TERRORISM, including acts
of terrorism transcending national boundaries,

BOLO-See CIA internal communication US9879-CT 5003,
02195WEP.

Description:
See original BOLO

Comment: Fugitive is an expert marksman, martial artist,
a master of disguises, and a pitiless killer capable of using
multiple lethal methods. He may have weaponized Marburg
Hemorrhagic Fever virus materials in his possession. He is
presumed to be heavily armed and willing to resort to violence at any instance in which his freedom is threatened. He
is extremely dangerous and should be approached only with
a JTF-6 or police swat team equivalent. He will not hesitate
to kill law enforcement officers or bystanders. Use of deadly
force is approved unless the fugitive complies with lawful com-
mands immediately.

Ed Simonsen took the podium.
"I'll be brief. We are going after him. He appears to have
gone back to roost in the Congo presuming that it is a safe-
haven for him. We have a small force of trusted Congolese

security forces and five agents from the Firm. In addition, I am going to take Dr. Norcroft with us. She has an uncanny ability to be in the right place and the right time and to do the right thing. I consider her to be my rabbit's foot."

Everyone laughed. They were all fully aware of the publicity the Wolf News medical consulted had generated and that it had proved to be highly beneficial thus far.

After the formal meeting concluded, Ed and Special Agent Walsh cornered Sybil.

"I hope I didn't speak out of school back there," Ed said.

"It was a bit presumptuous," Sybil said, "especially in view of how my husband feels; but I am determined to see this mission to the bitter end. I'll go. When?"

"Tomorrow, but first we need to get any information from your daughter, Cerisse, that we can. It is my bet that she knows a great deal about the on-the-ground people and places involved in Pourciau's criminal and terrorist enterprise in the DRC."

Sybil thought about it for a moment, "I guess it couldn't hurt to ask her a few questions, but let's go easy. She's still just a little girl who has been through a lot. I reserve the right to stop questioning if it seems to be getting to be too much for her."

The agents nodded.

Chapter Ten

Cerisse had a clear mind and was able to give the mission leaders a concise and accurate map of the area near the Fabrique Pharmaceutique DRC buildings and about camps where she and her pygmy girl-friends had so unfortunately been taken.

"They will hide here more likely than anywhere else," she said pointing to an X on her own map. "Don't worry about the pygmy people betraying you. They will soon recognize that you are there to help them. They hate the whites and the Bantu passionately because they are the slavers, rapists, and cannibals who hunt our people and eat them like wild animals. They will help if you let them."

Sybil was impressed at how rapidly her daughter's English was improving. She was proud of how grown up the little girl was becoming. Operating from a safe and protected base, she was able to give an unemotional and cogent argument about where the human traffickers and terrorists would most likely be and who was likely to be present in the hideout camps.

Ed and Grant Walsh put their agencies—the CIA and FBI—into high gear to block every known exit from the DRC for every known terrorist and human trafficker on the list. The DRC is bordered by the Central African Republic and South Sudan to the north; Uganda, Rwanda, and Burundi in the east; Zambia and Angola to the south; the Republic of the Congo, the Angolan exclave of Cabinda, and the Atlantic Ocean to the west; and is separated from Tanzania by Lake Tanganyika in the east. Every major port, airport, and highway was being monitored and road blocks were quietly put into place. The more precise effort was expended to create a cordon sanitaire around Goma, the town of Rutshuru, and every village within a three hundred mile circumference around the villages known to be heavily populated by pygmies or known to harbor pygmy slaves and prostitutes.

The members of the CIA and PNC [Congolese National Police] mission arrived five miles away from Rutshuru. Sybil was weighted down with a heavy pack of water, freeze-dried food, her Glock .30, and ammunition, a stringer of grenades, a combat K-bar knife, and medical supplies. She was tired from the long air trip from Washington's Andrews Air Force Base to Kinshasa and to Goma and then overland to the out-skirts of Rutshuru. But, she was exhilarated by the prospects of finally seeing the monster, Jean-Pierre Alain Pourciau, brought down.

Charles had demanded that she take with her a special, ultra-expensive satellite phone and that she call him multiple times every day to keep him and Cerisse in the loop—no long silences permitted. The plan was to move through the jungle around Rutshuru on foot and then to link up with a convoy of vehicles being brought in from the town of Gisenyi, Rwanda on the east, ostensibly trucking in heavy machine parts bound for Goma, Gisenyi's opposite village on the banks of Lake Kivu in the Congo. The machine parts were to be off loaded at the approach to the dirt track leading to the village of Sange and the well-armed police force loaded into the trucks for the final assault on their target village— St. Laurente de Paris—where Cerisse had said the terrorists would be hiding.

It was a two day trek through steaming jungles. Sweat poured off the members of the mission, and water became the most valuable commodity on earth by the time they came near to the dirt road that cut off to Sange. Along the way, they had been met by pygmy trackers who guided them through the often impenetrable dark forests. At the designated rendezvous point, they met the drivers of the truck convoy, all members of the *Medecins sans Frontieres*—Doctors Without Borders—who had been running, hiding from, and sometimes even fighting the majority Bantu confederates of the white slavers, pimps, and cannibals in order to bring some beneficial health measures to the wretched people of the forests. They did not want recognition, praise, or payment. They wanted secrecy above all; and, as in their many other endeavors, they were willing to face serious risks to help the poor people whom they regarded as their patient population.

"*Bonne journée, mes amis,*" the leader of the convoy said.

Sybil was the acknowledged linguist of the mission; so, she was elected to handle this part of the conversation. She responded in unaccented French.

"And to you, my friends. We hope you traveled in safety."

"We did. Do you think you can pull this grand design off, Doctor?"

Her reputation had preceded her.

"With your help, yes."

"Nothing better could happen in the Congo that to get rid of the monsters who instill such terror into the humble hearts of these unfortunate little people. We will leave you now and wish you the greatest good fortune. Call on us if we can be of more help."

With that, they turned back towards the relative safety of Gisenyi in the temporarily peaceful hapless country of Rwanda. The members of the mission waited an hour until a coterie of pygmy trackers and fighters arrived to lead them through the winding trails which skirted the main road into St. Laurente de Paris. Then they set off for their final destination, weapons locked and loaded.

Cerisse and her pygmy friends had been correct about the village and that it would be the stronghold for the slavers, pimps, and terrorists. Jean-Pierre Alain Pourciau, his six lieutenants, forty lower ranking white confederates, and fifty-one Bantu mercenary soldiers hired by the Fabrique Pharmaceutique DRC and paid by al Qaeda cadres, were sweating out their stay in the uncomfortable and malodorous little town. Their presence had overwhelmed the meager sanitary facilities and had diminished the clean water supply nearly to extinction so that baths were out of the question. Alcohol supplies were similarly depleted and that was a source of acrimony and contention.

The FBI, CIA, PNC, and pygmy forces silently gathered in the inky blackness of the rain forest surrounding the village which had originally been intended to be a respite location for Europeans who wanted to eat their own kind of food, drink European wines, and to have their way with defenseless little black women. The strident voices of angry men echoed through the trees, and there were frequent noises indicative of a hard fight in progress complete with bored men egging the antagonists on.

Things began to quiet down at midnight; and by two a.m., the town finally became quiet. Ed gave the signal—two clicks on a finger clacker that had come to the Congo from the LRRP forces who once fought in the jungles of Viet Nam. Otherwise, the circumferential influx of trained fighters closing in on the town was silent. Ed had ordered his men and Sybil to halt at the tree line before starting into the cleared area outside the buildings. The pygmies had secretly disarmed the landmines on a trail leading to the first buildings. Without that knowledge, the assault would have ended in a slaughter before the first law enforcement officer made it to the first building.

Ed, Sybil, Doug Mason, and two PNC commando officers made their way to the cabin known to house Pourciau and his top officers. Pygmy poison-tipped arrows dispatched three of the six sentries guarding the cabin. Two other guards were dead drunk, and the pygmies made them just dead. The last village guard was grabbed from behind by a powerful arm belonging to Ed Simonsen's second-in-command from the CIA contingent.

Sybil was ordered to stay outside of the cabin until Ed gave the all-clear. She obeyed with gratitude. It was a very frightening place and time. The others slipped silently into the sleeping area and chloroformed the sleepers who were already largely anesthetized by the alcohol overdose they had administered to themselves. They were all blindfolded with black hoods, their mouths duct-taped, and their wrists and ankles secured with flexicuffs. Ed radioed his other captains that the main targets had been secured without casualties and that they could now move in.

At first, several cabins full of snoring terrorists were secured in a similar fashion and without noise or casualties. With about twenty men left slumbering away in the last two cabins, the mission's charmed existence fell apart. A Bantu mercenary chose that time to relieve himself against the cabin wall and sounded an alarm to the rest of the camp when he saw the intruders. He died from a K-bar wound across his throat, and the remaining pygmies and their larger comrades rushed into the last cabins with guns ablaze. In three minutes it was all over, and twenty new corpses were created to fertilize the jungle floor.

Ed signaled the all-clear, and shortly the convoy of trucks drove freely into the village and collected the trussed, muffled, and blind-folded captives and loaded them unceremoniously into the beds of the trucks which were none-too-clean. Ed and the PNC officers searched the cabins and found half a truck load of incriminating documents.

Half an hour later, they torched the village and drove away. None of the mission participants had suffered anything more than a scratch from their march through the thick undergrowth of the jungle. Doug Mason got the greatest combat and police footage of his career. By the time the convoy reached Rutshuru, he was able to send off a lightly edited set of background videos—to erase the faces and any other identifiers of the CIA and PNC officers. Sybil gave her commentary for the filming surrounded by two dozen of her newest pygmy friends, all grinning and laughing for the pure joy of seeing the destruction of their centuries old tormentors.

Charles and Cerisse had seen Doug's handiwork and heard Sybil's delivery dozens of time before she arrived back home.

Charles was grudgingly complimentary but still insisted that Sybil find a safer way to carry on her work. Cerisse wept for joy from the reunion with her mother and because she and her mother had been instrumental in striking a heart-blow to the monsters who had so abused her and her little people for so long. Special Agent Grant Walsh called to let Sybil know another piece of good news. Pourciau's deadly box had been found in a duffel bag being carried by one of his men into New York's Grand Central Station. No one was hurt, and it appeared that the entire supply of the deadly Marburg virus that anyone had any knowledge about had been retrieved.

Chapter Eleven

David Kilcannon, vice-president of news coverage for Wolf News sought Sybil out after she taped a couple of "heroine-returns-back-to-home-base" stories.

"It's nuts, Sybil. You have put us on the world's news map. We are so many points higher than WWN that they can only sigh and hope that they will escape bankruptcy. But...you have not even been welcomed to the Wolf News channel with a proper interview. Barbara is ready anytime. How about doing it as a Sunday night special? That would mean taping tomorrow or the next day at the latest."

"Give me until next week. Hype it up for the week, and I am sure it will drive the viewership and ratings way up. I need to finish dealing with the victims and their treatment for a bit first. I am told that the rate of infections, treatment center admissions, and deaths are declining significantly; and there is real hope for an end to this man-made biological disaster. For one thing, I want to get the straight facts and to get some face-to-face footage with the movers and shakers from the CDC and other governmental agencies. Okay?"

It was a good plan; and, as usual, better than he had envisioned; so, David readily agreed.

The CDC's facts were grim, but did indicate that the epidemic was finally losing out to the army of specialists who were running the quarantine and treatment arms of the containment program for the Marburg virus scourge. The facts were that over 100,000 people of all ages, colors, and backgrounds had been infected; 69,492 had died; and another 15-20,000 people were expected to die before the end of the month. The Fabrique Pharmaceutique DRC buildings were razed by torches wielded by employees of the company itself which was mounting a P-R effort to regain its good name comparable to the efforts by BP after their oil spill on April 20, 2010. In the BP Oil Spill, more than 200 million gallons of crude oil was pumped into the Gulf of Mexico for a total of 87 days, making it the biggest oil spill in U.S. history. 16,000 total miles of coastline were affected. The company spent more than $94 million on advertising in the aftermath.

Sybil worked half-days in the CDC [Center for Disease Control] Special Pathogens and Bacteria Branch clinical tents around New York and Washington D.C. area. There were still a few terrified souls brought in with enlarged, tender spleens, bloodshot eyes; they were sullen and often aggressive. Inexperienced attendants saw them as ingrates and bullies. Sybil knew that they shortly would develop a flu-like illness which would soon become a worse flu than they could ever imagine and that it would not be long before they joined the hundreds of prostrate victims in serried rows of the sufferers in extremis and agony. After they began to bleed from everywhere, only one in a hundred would survive. Still, Sybil and the others got into the sweltering hazmat suits and shuffled in to try—usually in vain—to save a few. When a patient walked out of the treatment unit, it was a trigger for a birthday-like celebration. Unfortunately, even for many of the survivors, the horror was not over. Many had serious brain damage, liver disease that sometimes progressed to chronic hepatitis and even liver failure. Not a few became psychiatric basket-cases. Most were weak, and the men were impotent. The worst thing for Sybil and her fellow scientists and co-workers was that they were no closer to finding a means of prevention or a cure than the world was when the disease was first identified in 1967.

The steel-nerved doctor and world-renowned television personality caved in each evening when she went home. Cerisse often washed her feet and rubbed them with soothing lotion. Charles was solicitous and forgiving of almost any of her dark moods and listlessness. As the disease waned, so did Sybil's ennui. Doug Mason discontinued his relentless filming, and for Wolf News and the rest of the world, the intensity of the story faded away as do all stories.

Now, David Kilcannon and Barbara Welhelme—the famous and incisive interviewer of the world's most fascinating people—finally prevailed on Sybil to do a two-hour interview. She insisted that Cerisse be part of the event and that it be filmed in her Georgetown home.

Ms Welhelme greeted the television audience, "It has been an incredibly eventful half year since Wolf News's new senior medical consultant arrived on the scene. This interview was originally scheduled to be presented that first week, but events of world-changing importance intervened. I am sure that no one in the world with a television set is unaware of the Marburg epidemic or of Dr. Sybil Norcroft's pivotal role in the discovery and treatment of the epidemic and of her part in bringing an end to the bio-terrorist cell which visited this scourge of biblical proportions on innocent people all around the world.

"So, Dr. Norcroft, it's time for you to get your story out. I would like to start way back at the beginning, well before you stepped foot in Wolf News studios. Tell us about your early life and education."

Sybil gave a self-deprecating and frequently amusing account of growing up, becoming consumed with ambition to be a doctor and then a neurosurgeon. Barbara probed some into her struggle against the patriarchal hurdles she had to overcome and into her work with feminist organizations to help women like herself to be able to compete on a level playing field with the members of the opposite gender.

"It hasn't always been easy, I understand, Dr. Norcroft. To let us know more about the real you, why don't you tell us about your struggles with the malpractice attorney, Paul Bel Geddes."

"Let me be brief about that, Barbara. He was the plaintiff's attorney in multiple malpractice cases against me. His tactics were overtly and unabashedly sexist, and in all cases, the premise of the suits was determined by a judge or a jury to be spurious. In one case, my malpractice insurance company agreed that the plaintiff had no case; but they settled anyway because the cost of litigation was too high. If anyone is interested in further details and documentation, you can go to my website—Dr.Sybil@WolfNews.com."

"And issues got even more serious in your dealings with the famous malpractice attorney, isn't that right?"

"They certainly did. I suppose I should be timid and avoid bringing this out to the public, but I am sure an intrepid investigative reporter will ferret the facts out eventually. To demonstrate once and for all that I have nothing to hide, you all can find out the details on my website. For tonight, I will give you the highlights of the case of California vs Sybil Norcroft."

For twenty-five minutes, Sybil gave a straight-forward and objective narrative of having received yet another intention-to-sue letter from Bel Geddes, of her lapse of decorum in castigating him privately and publicly, and of the attorney's murder. He had been killed in his palatial Bel Aire mansion by a single shotgun blast to the back of his head and had been robbed of millions of dollars in cash and jewelry. She told Barbara and her spell-bound television audience that she was arrested largely because of her foolish outbursts, because her alibi seemed weak, and not insignificantly, due to her gender.

"When I was on the brink of being convicted and going to prison for the rest of my life or receiving a death sentence, a superb set of private detectives and LAPD Robbery-Homicide Division detectives who were relentless in establishing the truth. Lt. Burger burst into the court room just as the judge was to be handed the jury's verdict and demonstrated effectively that, in fact, a disgruntled former client of Mr. Bel Geddes had killed him out of a long seething anger and to commit a robbery."

"Sounds like a taut court-room drama film set in the glitter of Hollywood to me, Dr. Norcroft," Barbara quipped.

She and Sybil laughed.

After the commercial break, Barbara directed Sybil to recount—in her own words—the events that unfolded on her first day of work. Sybil explained about how she ended up in the Congo, how the horrors of enslavement of the pygmies was discovered, and how it was determined that the al Qaeda terrorists and their operative set out to infect a major percentage of the world's population with an incurable and highly infections organism.

"Don't be shy, Dr. Norcroft, let's get to the exciting stuff."

Sybil told the whole story except for leaving out the CIA's role. She lavished compliments on the many law-enforcement officers who participated in the eventually successful struggle, including a riveting story about the pursuit and final battle in the jungle. She lauded those who had died in the line of duty including the FBI, DCPD officers who perished during the battles. She ended this part of the narrative on a personal note.

"I owe a great deal to the help given the effort by the girl who became my daughter. Barbara, may I present Cerisse Daniels. She escaped with me from the Congo. I will not go into detail, but let me assure you that she suffered the fires of hell at the hands of slaver-drivers and human traffickers. It is the happiest thing in this whole difficult story that she is alive, well, and soaring in her education here with me and my husband in the safety of the United States. Cerisse, would you join us, please."

Barbara threw soft-ball questions to Cerisse who answered them with charm and a fetching French accent. She was tiny, and except for her nearly adult feminine figure could be mistaken for an eleven-year-old. Sybil pushed the questions a little closer to the human trafficking, prostitution, and mass murders of her defenseless people at the hands of Jean-Pierre Alain Pourciau.

Cerisse had been coached to avoid seriously disturbing details, but she fielded the questions with youthful dignity and an absence of self-pity that made her a media darling for months to come. She was invited to speak to forums on the subjects of maltreatment of children and human trafficking.

Sybil and Charles were careful to avoid over-exposure and having anyone dredge up pain producing memories. In an unusual atmosphere of respect and kindness, the media for the most part were gentle with the charming little girl.

Chapter Twelve

E d Simonsen called Sybil the week following the interview. "Nice job on the interview. I was as proud as I could be of Cerisse. She is a keeper."

"That she is, Ed. How are things with you?"

"I'm okay, but I am getting involved in an international problem that I think you might like to have a part in. This one would have to be less public; although, eventually, everything you do ought to see the light of day; and you can count on an exclusive. It is a Company operation; so, the higher-ups would have to review and okay anything written or transmitted as photos or videos."

"So, what is it?"

"This time, you need to be briefed by Langley. Can you come over to the main building at noon on Saturday?"

"I guess so. I'll tell you, Ed, I have to wonder about what I have already gotten myself into let alone what a new involvement would hold."

"Sybil, you know that no one is going to force you in any way to do anything you don't want. However, you can't get insider information without more commitment. Hold off on your judgment until you hear what the *jefes* have in mind."

"Okay, I'll see you Saturday."

Sybil was nervous about what the CIA had in mind that involved her. She was well aware of the secrecy policies of the intelligence Company; so, she decided not to tell Charles what she was up to. He would never approve anyway. On Saturday morning she drove to the front gates of the CIA compound and gave her name to the gate guard. He checked the daily appointment log and opened the gates for her. He gave her directions, "so you won't have to wander around."

The receptionist handed her a visitors pass to hang around her neck and asked her to wait for an escort. While she waited, she glanced at the wall of black stars opposite her and was sure that the lowest one appeared newer than the rest. She presumed that it belonged to the late Dirk Ravens, and she felt a brief pang of sadness.

"Follow me, please," a giant of a man in uniform said.

He led her to the fourth floor to a room marked "COU." The plot was beginning to thicken, and Sybil became even more nervous. The escort knocked three times and waited for a response. When he heard, "Enter", he opened the door and indicated to Sybil to go in.

Ed Simonsen—whom she knew—and two other men were seated around a utilitarian desk. There were locked metal filing cabinets and a small table with a map on it, but no other indications of what went on in there.

"Welcome to the Covert Operations Unit. We're pretty informal here; mind if I call you Sybil? I'm John," the elder of the two officers said.

"Nice to meet you, Mr. Smith—I mean, John," Sybil said with a friendly smile.

John laughed out loud, "I think you've seen too many spy movies, Sybil."

He was in his early sixties, Sybil thought, but had a hard topographical face lined by squinting into the sun for years. He was wiry, and his movements were spare and efficient. His tanned face had what looked like a German dueling school scar diagonally across his left cheek. Between him and Ed was a man who—except for having black curly hair—looked very much like Ed. Sybil presumed they had been cut out from the same dough by the same cookie cutter. Both men were muscular and lean. Both had earnest eyes that betrayed nothing—one blue-eyed and the other hazel. They, like Sybil, waited until the man who had not been introduced or John spoke.

"I'm Erik, Sybil. And my last name is not Smith," Ed's companion said, and he and Sybil shared a short friendly laugh.

"I know you're busy; so, we'll get right to it," Erik said. "We have been following you for the great work you have been doing that involved the Company and for all you do to get objective news out and for the help in shutting down the Marburg virus epidemic. In fact, the director has given me the pleasure of showing you this commendation."

She looked at the simply worded document and smiled her thanks.

"Unfortunately, you can't keep it. The operations in which you were involved are still classified."

"Thanks…I guess," she said.

"We have a proposition to make to you. Before we do, I'm afraid you will have to sign the Official Secrecy Act documents. That okay?"

"I suppose. I am pretty much in the dark, and I was told that I would not have to do anything I don't want to do."

"You were informed correctly. This is not a contract; that would come later if you and the Company come to an agreement of just what you might do for your country."

She signed the documents which made it crystal clear that it was a serious felony for her to divulge secrets and that she would have to have anything she meant to communicate outside those people with an authorized need-to-know fully approved by the brass on the upper floors.

"All right. We have in mind a fairly long-term agency mission to interrupt the criminal individuals, companies, political groups, and governments who engage in human trafficking. Does that sound like something you would like to participate in?"

"Most definitely."

"We'll expedite all the paper work, and then we can fill you in on everything you need to know and what you can contribute. You will have to sign on as a contract agent with the CIA and take a lie-detector test before you can learn any more than what we've told you today. Any qualms?"

"No, I have nothing to hide."

Sybil found it very trying, this new requirement to keep secrets. She was a well-trained physician whose ethic and practice had always been to share her knowledge with her fellow scientists and clinicians. David Kilcannon pressed her to find out what she had been up to, but she was adamant about not revealing anything she might or might not be doing.

"The only thing I can say is that the stories I will be working on will require quite a bit of travel. My informants will have to remain confidential, and it will likely take quite a while before I can report on my activities. I will need to take Doug Mason along with me. We work well together and are a good team."

Doug had been vetted by the CIA along with her and was privy to everything she knew. Her first official journey abroad was scheduled for ten days later, and she and Doug were to meet Ed Simonsen in Vienna when they arrived.

Ed caught Sybil's eye and walked towards the Egyptair ticket counter.

"Book a round-trip ticket on flight 2260 for Cairo. I will be on the flight as well, but don't communicate with me. I'll see you there."

When they landed at CAI [Cairo International Airport], Sybil and Doug were met in the arrival lounge by two army officers who invited the Americans to accompany them. They were led to a black stretch Mercedes limo where the driver was standing at attention waiting to open the rear door for them. An Egyptian army brigadier general shifted in his seat to make room.

He said, "Welcome to Egypt. My name is Koffi Serge Elsayed Mukywana Muhanad. As is our custom in Egypt, I am usually known as Koffi Serge Muhanad—the last name was that of my father."

The powerful vehicle surged forward.

"It is an opportune time for you to come here to start your mission. Since the army removed the Muslim Brotherhood cabal who stole the election, things had begun to return to normal. It was a grim time for women and girls, and the army, under Col. Gen. Abasi. His name means "stern", and he is certainly that. He has set a goal of gender equality within 18 months. Still, there is considerable resistance to the concept. The Brotherhood has frightened the people into believing that it is Allah's will that women and girls be subjugated, and it will take time to undo the harm the Brotherhood has done."

"What about human trafficking and forced sexual slavery, honor killings, female genital mutilation, General?" Sybil asked, ignoring the CIA white papers she had been given that told her to tread lightly and to talk around subjects rather than proceeding directly.

"That is why you are here, and in fact, why we requested your participation in our program with the help of your CIA—Mr. Edmondsen there."

During the smooth ride to Field HQ, Heliopolis, Central Military Region, Gen. Muhanad discussed Sybil's pivotal role. She listened and agreed that the best approach would be to present herself in a well-publicized public persona as the Wolf News senior medical consultant who was an expert in biological terrorism. She would give dozens of speeches around the country about her exciting experiences in the Marburg virus interdiction program.

Behind the scenes, she would meet with army personnel, non-Muslim religious leaders, local and national secular leaders and the many opposition parties who applauded the ouster of the Muslim Brotherhood. She was already regarded as something of a Joan of Arc, and the people who opposed Islamization were prepared to gather behind her banner as soon as she could convince them that the United States and well-intentioned Europeans were ready to finance the efforts to protect females.

She would also have to convince them that military aid would be made available in the event that al Qaeda and the Brotherhood launched an armed insurrection against the

Egyptian forces for moderation. For all practical purposes, it would be a fact-finding political stump which had to be carried out largely in secret until sufficient evidence and a large enough population base was established to go public around the world. That is where the Wolf News medical consultant and photographer would be of paramount importance.

At headquarters, they met Col. Gen. Abasi briefly; but long enough for him to give Sybil, Doug, and Ed his full blessing.

"It is in the interest of myself and my like-minded countrymen to help you to succeed. We will provide a significantly large and powerful security guard that you will be safe and the message will be delivered that the government of Egypt and its defense forces are fully in agreement with what you are doing. May Allah guide your way and give you strength and endurance, my friends. I am sure that you will need it."

Sybil's first public appearance was held in the Cairo International Convention and Exhibition Center, and the ballrooms where she spoke were filled to overflowing. The *Cairo Daily News* and *Al Jazeera English News* gave long print columns to her fascinating adventure story and applauded the world-wide effort to rid itself of the Marburg scourge. She gave four television interviews the next morning then left the public eye, ostensibly to get a well-needed rest.

As a deliberate test, she, Ed, and Doug were flown immediately to Fayoum, about 60 miles south of Cairo, which is a well-known Brotherhood stronghold. Supporters of the new army-controlled government and security forces had been alerted in advance, and nearly a million of them gathered throughout the city plazas and main thoroughfares within the area where the amplified sound of Sybil's voice could reach. In that incendiary prone backwater, Sybil Norcroft took the risks and detailed what she know about FGM, enslavement, human trafficking, maltreatment, and neglect of women and girls. She was so well known throughout the Muslim and Egyptian world that she inspired instant trust. She implored the throng to rise up and to make a change that would last forever for females.

As soon as she finished her first public address, bullets began to fly; and the security forces hurried her away to the next engagement and then on to the next town. That scenario was repeated four times that day. The same plan unfolded in Alexandria and its nearby suburb of Borg Al-Arab which was a hot-bed of Brotherhood extremism—and on to the Nile Delta provincial city of Damietta. In each city, Sybil met with pre-vetted leaders who were committed to bringing about the end of the worst of the outrages against women. Everywhere she went, she was greeted with enthusiasm and often with skirmishes between the Islamists and Egyptian security forces.

A sniper put a bullet hole in the brim of her boonie hat, a fact she vowed never to tell her husband about. An army sergeant-major ambushed and killed the sniper—which was duly recorded with the Wolf News digital camera. Doug Mason dutifully filmed all the progress, and he and Sybil recorded ten for-television interviews which were sent to an unknown location controlled by the CIA for later public presentation.

The following day, Sybil was shrouded in a burka and taken to where a female circumcision was to be performed. Four little girls were brought reluctantly into the center of an open concrete plaza encircled by a ring of crumbling tenements. There Doug faithfully recorded every ghastly bit of inhumanity—all the blood, the screaming, the fainting, and the unbearable destruction of the genitals of the innocent children. One little girl died screaming; the stress of the fear and pain were more than her young heart could tolerate. It was all Sybil could do to restrain herself, knowing that the record she was making would be far more influential in helping save other girls. That Sybil enjoyed such prominence was going to make the difference.

Later in the day, Sybil interviewed women and girls who were in hiding to save themselves from honor killings. Others told of having fingers clipped off for minor offenses or for refusing to permit themselves to be sold into physical or sexual slavery. Three of the young women she interviewed had suffered amputations of ears, noses, and one was blinded by acid—all because they had refused to marry elderly men selected by their fathers, who received handsome financial rewards for sacrificing their daughters' virginity.

The next day was to be a replay of the day before but in a different city. It was uncomfortable but peaceful until she met with the council of elders where were not sympathetic to the outside interference by what they considered to be anti-Islamic activists. Sybil had not gotten through her first sentence—one she had memorized in Egyptian—when a suicide bomber was stopped in the open area outside the meeting tent. He was shot by security guards which caused his bomb to explode killing himself and two guards. Had he gotten thirty feet closer, Sybil and her entourage would have been nothing but bits of DNA to be processed. A screaming band of Brotherhood extremists burst into the neighborhood firing their automatic weapons in the direction of the meeting tent.

The first volleys killed five elders—all sympathizers with the invading Islamists. Everyone else hit the floor and began firing out through the tent openings. Sybil fired five magazines of bullets from her personal Glock .30, picked up the first of three discarded AK-47s and held off the first attack force to get close enough to the tent to menace everyone in it. Doug Mason got chillingly gripping footage of the beautiful

American blond woman killing six of the attackers, calmly dropping her empty cartridge magazine and putting in a fresh one, then repeating the process two more times.

Within minutes, the terror was over; and the Egyptian army guards began the mopping up process. That consisted of killing all of the wounded combatants and half a dozen fleeing killers. It made for deeply stirring digital film coverage, but neither Sybil nor Doug Mason believed that any of that filming would ever see the public light of day.

Sybil was a disheveled mess, but that only contributed to the heroic image she was presenting. It would be marvelous coverage and a commercial bonanza for the previously struggling Wolf News network channel. When things settled down, Ed rushed to her side and asked how she was doing.

"Okay, but maybe it wouldn't be a bad idea to act like ducks and get the flock outta here," she said calmly—more calmly than she felt inside.

The word had gotten around and every place they landed in the seven Muslim countries they visited was ignited into a firefight with considerable carnage. Sybil bemoaned what was happening, but the army officers and Ed assured her that this would turn the world's attention to the problem of human trafficking and abuses of females like nothing in history had ever done.

She was in the Middle-East for a total of three months. With the exception of a safe respite in Israel for five days, Sybil Norcroft, M.D., Ph.D., F.A.C.S., the sophisticated, urbane, peace-loving, neurosurgeon cum television personality, was under fire. She knew that her presence had started a minor war, but she consoled herself that it was a war that needed to begin. She did not apologize for nor repent of her role in the beginning of the epic struggle. And she gradually morphed into a warrior.

Chapter Thirteen

When Sybil finally returned to the United States and the safe havens of her home in Georgetown and her workplace in the heart of New York City, she learned that she had become a media star comparable to any movie personality who was ever hyped by the Hollywood machine. David Kilcannon took over her schedule to avoid over-exposure and exhaustion. The channel had a serious vested interest in their rising iconic medical consultant. They wanted her to be as safe as her perpetually worried husband, Charles Daniels, and her daughter, Cerisse, did.

If it could be said that Sybil's celebrity had gone viral or atmospheric before the CIA permitted the raw footage of the firefights and the stirring exhortations and debates Sybil had starred in to be made public, then the more recent celebrity status could only be described as stratospheric.

While riding the crest of that wave, Sybil received a request that she come to the Office of the Surgeon General for a visit.

General Lopez greeted her with genuine admiration and fondness, "Dr. Norcroft, you have been brilliant. I hope it won't all go to your head. You know fame fades. I believe you have the character and integrity to withstand the onslaught of the hype-makers."

"I have been able to do so thus far, General. I was never cut out for all of this adulation and attention. How should I handle what has been created?"

"Be yourself. Remember your mission. The president and I are fully aware of your involvement with the CIA and the intelligence and security forces of Egypt and the other Muslim countries who are trying to raise the standards of health for women in their countries. We applaud you for what you have done. This is like a huge social poker game. The question—as the singer, Kenny Rogers, sang in his song, *The Gambler*—is "If you're gonna play the game, boy, ya gotta learn to play it right. You got to know when to hold 'em, know when to fold 'em, Know when to walk away and know when to run. You never count your money when you're sittin' at the table. There'll be time enough for countin' when the dealin's done…"

Sybil laughed with the Surgeon General who knew that he had a terrible off-key singing voice.

"I'm sure there's real truth in that," she said.

"I presume that you realize that I did not invite you here to be subjected to an abysmal musical performance."

"So, why did you?" Sybil asked cutting to the heart of the conversation.

"Well, my dear, in truth, I did not do the inviting. The president of the United States did. He wanted to have me feel you out before you made a public appearance at the White Office. He is considering offering you position, and wants to know if you would give it consideration."

"What position?"

"I am sworn to secrecy, but it is a fine addition to your already amazing curriculum vitae. I can tell you that much. How about it?"

"Why not? I came this far. What is next?"

The surgeon general gave her the specifics. She was to meet the president in the Oval Office in 48 hours.

Sybil had—by now—arrived at a point in her career that her head was not easily turned. She surprised herself at how comfortable she was becoming in the rarified atmosphere of media stardom and now with an invitation to meet with President Willets alone. She did pause to wonder what her proud father and mother would have said had they lived long enough to see this week in her life.

The surgeon general had smoothed the process of getting into the White House. Sybil arrived ten minutes early to be sure she would not be unduly held up by the security measures. As it turned out, his name, her name, and the appointment time were all that was needed to move her through the process; so, she was standing before the president's secretary with five minutes to spare.

Erin Novak looked up at Sybil at the exact second of her appointment time, "The president will see you now, Dr. Norcroft."

The president himself opened the Oval Office door and invited her in. She had seen innumerable photographs, videos, television depictions, and movies of the famous power room; but the in-person three dimensional experience still afforded her a thrill.

"Thank you for taking time to see me, Dr. Norcroft. You are probably the best known woman in the country, perhaps the world; but it is still a pleasure to be able to shake your hand."

His grip was firm, even personal; and he looked her in the eye. He was tall, greying, and handsome—something of the charisma of John F. Kennedy emanated from the man and drew her in—as it did his huge constituency base. His dark-grey suit and blue-grey tie on a white shirt— that looked as if he changed shirts three times a day—were perfectly matched to the color of his precisely coiffed hair.

"The pleasure is mine," Sybil said.

He gestured to her to sit on a coach on the left side of the room while he took his seat on the right. It was the perfect homey touch—inviting, reassuring, direct eye-to-eye-contact and yet maintained the distance that his power contributed to his side of the room.

"I know you are busy; so, I'll get down to the reason I invited you here. Actually, there are two reasons, but I will hold off on the second until another, more formal time. Dr. Norcroft, my administration wishes to present you with the Presidential Medal of Freedom. I am sure you realize that it is the highest award the country offers to a civilian. You are certainly worthy of the honor."

Sybil was dumbfounded, thrilled, amazed, delighted, humbled, and a bit frightened at the prospect. She paused before answering.

"Mr. President, I don't know what to say. It is an honor that I would never have dreamt of, let alone have had the temerity to covet…Thank you."

"It is my place to thank you. You know how politics and media coverage are. I am embarrassed to have to ask you a few questions so that neither of us is ever embarrassed by something being revealed that we did not anticipate. Are you all right with that?"

"Yes, Sir. I presume that every bit of your life and all of your decisions come under magnified scrutiny. I certainly do not take any offense of the need to be straightforward with you. What's first?"

First, he asked a few telling questions about her past history—any radical associations, hidden criminal acts, regrettable public communications, etc. Next, he delved into the history of her having been indicted, tried, and found not guilty of murder. Finally, he asked only a couple of questions about her political leanings to be sure that there were not going to be any undisclosed skeletons in her closet. He was satisfied with all of her answers.

"Thank you for being so candid, Doctor. I think it unlikely that we will hear any protests from the public or the press except for those who are still biased against the LGBT community which you defend so regularly. It is a disappointment to me as president to have to admit that there are still racists, sexists, ageists, and religious bigots in our country. I admire how you have handled yourself as you have gone about supporting the issues in which you believe."

"Mr. President, you said there were two reasons why you wanted me to come here today. Any hints?"

"Forgive the drama and the secrecy, Dr. Norcroft, but what I have in mind for you requires secrecy. And, I'm sorry to have to warn you that—should you agree to get into the area where I am going—you will have to be more thoroughly vetted than you could ever have imagined. All I can tell you now is that you will need to have an ultra-top secret security clearance. Still want to go on and satisfy your curiosity?"

She shook her head, "yes" and both of them laughed at the turgid theater of his statement with its oblique reference to secrets while agreeing that it was probably altogether necessary.

-The End-

AUTHOR CARL DOUGLASS, a former neurosurgeon turned full time author, writes with gripping realism because in all his books he has been there and done that in some measure. He grew up in a small town where fighting was the rule, not the exception. He was determined to escape the sameness of geography, intellectual outlook, and career prospects of the majority of his contemporaries. In complete naiveté, he applied to only one well-known major university for his undergraduate work, and to everyone's surprise, he was accepted. He found himself out of his league scholastically and had to work like a Hannibal to find a way or make one to succeed in that rarefied atmosphere. His goal of success was to become a neurosurgeon, and he did it. His career in academia and the military as well as his work as a medical humanitarian provided the background to produce the riveting tales that have made their way into his remarkable books.

HONORS, AWARDS, AND MEMBERSHIPS
Phi Kappa Phi University Honor Society
Alpha Omega Alpha Medical Honor Society
BS (Medical Biology) degree—magna cum laude
MD—magna cum laude
CDR/MC/USN

American Medical Association
American Association of Neurosurgeons
Congress of Neurological Surgeons
Fellow of the American College of Surgeons
The Association of Military Surgeons of the United States
Life Member of the Medical Society of Vienna
Diplomate of the American Board of Neurological Surgery

Past President, Our Community Foundation, Wasatch
County, Utah
Past Medical Liaison Officer, Deseret International Founda-
tion
Past Chief of Surgery,
Antelope Valley Regional Medical Center, Lancaster, Cali-
fornia
Past Member-at-Large, Central Medical Committee,
Utah Valley Regional Medical Center, Provo, Utah
Past Member, Utah State Foster Care Review Committee

Sybil Norcroft Book Three

Secrets

In *Secrets*, Dr. Sybil Norcroft feels as if she has gotten in over her head in a welter of secrets and conflicts. She undergoes a lie detector test, gets a major national award, and gets inveigled into a secret association with the CIA, all in a dizzyingly brief period of time. She used to think her career as a practicing neurosurgeon was serious; but, after she is vetted for her CIA position, she gains a new appreciation for "serious." The director asks her, "After you are actively engaged in Company work, failing the lie detector test may mean a Company trial and swift and sure justice—the least noxious being dismissal. Any questions about the seriousness of that kind of justice?" Sybil felt chilly after completing that line of questioning. Her first assignment is to hack into the Russian president's computer system. The second assignment is to kill a man. What on earth has this nice lady from California gotten herself into?